MURDER
ON THE
CLOCK

BOOKS BY LUCY CONNELLY

MERCY MCCARTHY MYSTERIES
An Irish Bookshop Murder
Death by the Book
Death at Inishmore Castle

MURDER ON THE CLOCK

Lucy Connelly

Bookouture

Published by Bookouture in 2025

An imprint of Storyfire Ltd.
Carmelite House
50 Victoria Embankment
London EC4Y 0DZ

www.bookouture.com

The authorised representative in the EEA is Hachette Ireland
8 Castlecourt Centre
Dublin 15 D15 XTP3
Ireland
(email: info@hbgi.ie)

ISBN: 978-1-83618-922-0
eBook ISBN: 978-1-83618-921-3

Thank you, Steve, for believing in me.

ONE

As I stared at my computer screen, I very much wanted to bang my head on my keyboard with frustration. Instead of working on my latest novel, I'd spent the better part of two hours searching for birthday gift ideas for my twin, Lizzie. She always gave such thoughtful presents.

Whereas I was more of a 'throw a gift certificate in a card' kind of person. But this was our first birthday without our mom, who was also a great gift-giver, and I wanted to do something special for her.

I groaned. "It shouldn't be this hard."

"Mercy, after all the books you've written, I'd think you would have figured it out by now," Lizzie said from the doorway. She grinned.

I laughed, and popped my latest manuscript on the screen so she couldn't see what I'd been looking at. "I keep telling you, it never gets any easier," I said.

Mr. Poe, who had been curled up in his dog bed in front of the fireplace in my office, grunted as if we'd disturbed him. Even though it was close to summer, there was a chill in the air in

Shamrock Cove, Ireland. It was also very wet. I kept a fire going in my office most of the day and he loved sleeping in front of it.

I glanced at my watch and then frowned. "I had no idea it was time for lunch."

"That's why you have me," she said. "I left you a sandwich and some strawberry pie in the fridge. Don't forget to eat."

"Pie?" I stood.

She laughed like that was the funniest thing in the world.

"I knew that would catch your interest. You're an adult and can do what you want, but maybe eat the sandwich first."

"We'll see. Are you heading back to the bookstore?" We'd inherited our grandfather's bookshop in this small Irish town. She ran it like the pro she was. Once she set her mind to something, she always succeeded. But she was also the kindest human being I knew.

"I am. I thought I might see if Mr. Poe wanted to come with me, but it's pouring outside, and he looks quite comfy."

He grunted again, and then put his paws over his eyes, as if he were hiding.

"I can take a hint," she said. "Do you mind taking him on his afternoon walk? The rain is supposed to pause in a few hours."

"I don't mind at all. We could probably both use a stretch."

"Okay, I'll see you later."

After eating the strawberry pie and sandwich in that order, an idea hit me. Mr. Poe followed me to my bedroom, and I opened my jewelry box. In the bottom of it, I found a watch that had belonged to my mother. She'd never worn it, and we hadn't seen it until we'd been going through her things after she died.

It was an old Rolex, and had a diamond facet, but it no longer worked. There was an inscription that read: 'To my greatest love.' We had no idea who had given it to Mom, but we assumed it was our father. A man we'd never met. A man we suspected might be very much alive and living somewhere in Ireland.

At least, we hoped that was true. Though, if he was alive, why hadn't he contacted us? That was the biggest mystery of our lives.

We'd both loved the watch, but my sister had taken several of Mom's diamond rings, so she'd told me to keep it. But I'd seen the way she looked at it. I had other watches—some really nice ones my publisher had bought me. Giving her the watch would mean a lot to her.

The item no longer worked, but maybe it just needed a battery. I stuffed it into the pocket of my jeans.

"Come on, Mr. Poe. Time for our walk."

He grudgingly rose from his bed and sat perfectly straight while I put on his plaid harness. It had stopped raining, but I grabbed an umbrella and pulled on my dark-green wellies. One could never be sure here that it wouldn't pour down buckets of rain at any moment.

While it might have bothered some people, I loved it. The gloominess made for perfect writing weather.

We left Number 3 Hidden Way Lane, our Tudor-style cottage tucked into the court. It was a fairy-tale neighborhood with beautiful gardens, and five other thatched-roof cottages. Our neighbors had become some of our best friends the last few months and we loved living here. Making the move from the States had been a big one, but we'd settled in nicely.

After pushing through the hidden door in the stone wall that surrounded the cottages, we walked up the back alley a bit and then turned at the corner to head to Main Street. The clock shop was on the corner across the street from the side our bookstore was on. Thankfully, our store was half a block down. Otherwise, my sister might have seen me.

There was a clock-shaped sign hanging on an iron hanger. The sign read: Flynn & Flynn, Clocks & Repair.

Mr. Poe and I walked in, and a brass bell tinkled overhead. Almost every store on Main Street had some version of that bell.

My sister thought it was the most charming security system around.

"Afternoon," Declan Flynn said from behind a glass counter, which held a wealth of treasures from rings and watches to crystal figurines and necklaces. The walls on all sides were covered in all kinds of clocks. There were cuckoos and even a few grandfather clocks in the corners. "How can we help you today, Ms. McCarthy?" His heavy Irish brogue made me smile.

He was handsome with dark hair that swooped over one brow, and a bright white smile. He wore a long-sleeved button-down and jeans. But the shirt was untucked giving him a roguish look.

"Hi again, Declan," I said. "I told you to call me Mercy." I'd come in a few times with the clocks our grandfather had collected to have them given a once-over. We wanted to keep the contents of the cottage working well in honor of him.

Mr. Poe grunted. He had not been properly greeted.

"Afternoon, young man." He waved toward Mr. Poe. "He looks quite fierce today."

"That's his 'do you have a treat for me look'," I said.

"Sorry, fella. No treats here."

We'd said the 'T' word twice and presented nothing. He grunted again. He really was a funny little guy.

"You don't mind if he comes in with me, do you?"

"All are welcome," said the elder Mr. Flynn, who had white hair. He sat at a desk with a giant magnifying glass and a pair of tweezers. He was fixing something and didn't bother to look up.

"Dad is right," Declan said. "All are welcome. What can we help you with today?"

I pulled the watch from my pocket. "I'd like to get this fixed up for a gift. It hasn't worked in years. Well, I don't think it has. I inherited it from my mom, and she never wore it. And I'm babbling. Anyway, I want to fix it up for my sister.

Our birthday is coming up soon. Can you do that sort of thing?"

"My da can fix anything," he said.

"Don't be braggin' on, my boyo. Bring it here." While his tone was grumpy, the older man smiled to take the edge off his words.

Declan handed his father the watch. After turning it over and then tapping it a few times, he listened to it. Since it wasn't working, I had no idea what he might hear.

"We can fix her up," Flynn senior said. "Have it ready for you in two days or so. My son will contact you." Then he went back to whatever he was working on.

I laughed, as did his son. "And that is why he has me to work the front of the shop," Declan said. "He tends to get involved with whatever he's working on and forgets everything else."

"I'm not deaf," the older gentleman said.

"Never said you were, Da. Anyway, leave it with us. Do you need a quote, though?"

I shrugged.

"Da? How much?"

"Don't know what all it will take, do I now? But less than four hundred for an overhaul. May be a bit more if I need parts."

That sounded perfectly reasonable to me. "Okay, great. Thank you. See you soon."

Mr. Poe and I strolled down the colorful Main Street to the beach at the end of the lane. There were a few people sitting out in chairs. I thought it was a bit cool for that sort of thing, and just as I was thinking that the sun came out.

I took the harness off Mr. Poe and let him chase the waves. He was careful not to get wet though.

I sat on a rock that made up part of the long jetty that went out into the sea and watched him play. It was a bit noisier than usual, as men and women built temporary booths for the upcoming summer fête. My sister was involved in the committee, and there were all sorts of rides, artists and food on the way. Shamrock Cove liked a good party, or fête as they called them here. And this one was for the opening of the tourist season.

By the time Mr. Poe was done scaring the waves away, we were both tired.

As we passed the bookstore, he insisted we go inside and visit my sister. While I knew he loved me, and I him, she was definitely his person. The store was crowded, which seemed odd for a Thursday afternoon. But he ran around the front counter, and she scooped him up.

"Someone has been playing near the sea," she said.

"That he has. What's going on?" I whispered across the counter.

"Oh, I forgot to tell you. It's the ladies who lunch crowd. They've started a new book club, which meets here two Thursdays a month. Lolly's idea, of course."

Lolly was our neighbor, and the grand dame of the town. She was lovely, narcoleptic—a condition where she could fall into a deep sleep when in relaxing surroundings—and people tended to do whatever she told them. And she was the grandmother of the local detective inspector, Kieran. We adored her.

"Do you need any help?" I asked.

"No. I'm good. Caro is here to help with checkouts."

"You sure?"

She nodded.

"Okay. Mr. Poe, you ready to go?"

She held him over her shoulder, and he snuggled into her neck. "He can stay here with me. You get to work."

"I see how it is, Mr. Poe." I smirked.

"Hey, he spent all morning with you. This is my time with the best pup in the world." He snuggled even closer.

We laughed.

"I can tell when I'm not needed. I'll see you later."

"Hey, don't forget the pub quiz tonight."

"I won't." I already had. So, I made a note in my phone and set an alarm to remind me to get ready.

A few hours later, we met our friends from the court at the Crown and Clover pub. Rob, Scott, Brenna, and Lolly were all on our team, and were our neighbors on the court. Rob and Scott were married. Rob was a chef and Scott a computer programmer. Brenna was a photographer, who did a lot of work for magazines, with the occasional side gig in glamorous parts of the world. She'd just returned from Dubai.

We'd all become very close the last few months. Between us, we all had our strengths for the pub quiz, and we'd won more than once.

Our friend Matt, and his mom, the pub owners, took turns calling out the questions. They let us bring Mr. Poe inside and had made the pub dog friendly. And we loved them for it. Mr. Poe went just about everywhere with us, as neither Lizzie nor I could resist his sad puppy dog eyes.

While we all had our heads together examining a picture quiz a fight broke out in the corner.

"Who is that?" Mercy asked.

Lolly shook her head. "That's just the Donnels. They like their drink a bit too much and argue over the smallest things. Best to ignore them." She gave them one of her Lolly looks of disdain. It was all I could do not to laugh.

During one of the breaks, Scott went off to get us another round of drinks.

"So, we were going to do it as a surprise, but then we were worried you two might make other plans," Brenna said.

I wasn't a huge fan of surprises. "What do you mean?" I asked.

"We're throwing you a birthday party a week from Saturday. Just a few friends. But we aren't telling you when or where until the day."

"You don't have to do that," Lizzie said. She sounded nervous. I was usually the one who wasn't a party person. But she had anxiety, which sometimes manifested when she was wary of something.

"Oh, we do. You know how we love a party," Rob interjected. He took Lizzie's hands in his. "I promise it is something you will both love."

She grinned and then nodded.

"Please assure me that there won't be costumes?" I asked, dreading the truth.

"You'll just have to go along with whatever we do because you love us and you trust us," Rob said.

I sighed. "I suppose."

They all laughed.

We came in second for the pub quiz. We'd lost out because there were several sports questions. Those usually fell to our friend, Detective Inspector Kieran O'Malley. He'd been called out on a case and had to cancel last minute.

We were talking and laughing on the walk back to the court. Just as we were about to turn and head to our place, I noticed something out of the corner of my eye.

The lamppost across the street was out again. That happened more than once with the old gas lights.

I stopped but my friends kept going.

"Mercy, what's wrong?" Rob asked. They must have realized I had paused.

"Does it look like the door to the jewelry shop is open? What if someone broke in?"

"Is that your writer's brain or do you really see something?"

he asked. The others seemed to notice we'd stopped, and they backtracked.

"I think the door is open to the jewelry store, but I can't see clearly. I'm going to check it out."

"We're coming with you," Scott and Rob said.

The whole group crossed the street together. The door was open, and it was dark inside. The wind caught it, and it was obvious there was glass on the floor.

"Someone call 999," I said.

I pulled out the mace I carried in my bag. A woman who lived in New York never went anywhere without it. At least, that held true for me. I turned on the flashlight app on my phone.

Inside, our feet crunched on the broken glass. "Don't touch anything," I said. "It looks like a burglary."

"What if they are still here?" Lizzie whispered from the doorway.

"I don't think so. They wouldn't have left the door open if they were still inside."

There was a moaning sound. Rob and I glanced at each other in the dark. Then he followed me around the counter.

On the floor was the elder Mr. Flynn.

I rushed to him and put two fingers on his neck.

"Is he alive?" Rob whispered.

"Barely," I answered, as I started CPR.

TWO

My friends and I waited for Detective Inspector Kieran O'Malley and his team at the clock shop. It didn't seem right to leave with the door wide open. When we couldn't find a pulse, I'd started CPR and Rob had helped with the chest compressions. Before the emergency folks arrived, the Mr. Flynn senior had a pulse, but it was light. There was also some blood on his head.

The emergency techs had just rushed Mr. Flynn out of the store.

The flashing lights outside announced Kieran's arrival. He and I had a twice-a-week standing coffee date. He would come over and we'd talk about my work and his cases. Though, he never told me everything. But it was great having someone to brainstorm with about my books. We'd had a rocky beginning of our friendship, but now there was a mutual respect. I'd helped solve a few of his cases, and he shared info to show how grateful he was.

We all stood outside the clock shop as he approached.

"Grandson, I'm exhausted," Lolly said. "The ambulance has taken poor Mr. Flynn. Do you know how to contact his family?"

"I'll take care of the notifications, Gran," he said. "I'll need to talk with all of you, though. I'll try to make it quick. Give me a few minutes here."

"Are you sure? I can walk you through how we all ended up here," I said.

He nodded. "Okay, Mercy. You wait here. The rest can head home."

My sister opened her mouth and then closed it. As she turned away, I swore I saw her smile. "I'll put the kettle on," she said.

"We'll walk Lolly home and then hang out with Lizzie until you finish," Scott offered. He and Rob were always looking out for us. I honestly don't know what we would do without our sweet friends on the court.

"I won't have much to add, but you know where to find me," Lolly said. "Our Mercy was heroic once again. She brought him back from the dead, so she did."

"Rob helped," I said.

"Only because you told me exactly what to do," he said.

"Okay, I need to get on here. I'll be by later," Kieran said to our group.

Lizzie leaned into me. "You sure you don't want to come with us?"

"It's fine. Best to tell him everything while it's fresh in my memory."

She kissed my cheek. "You are a hero."

I snorted.

After they left, Kieran waved toward the doorway. "Why don't you take me through it?"

"We were walking home, and I noticed the door was open. When we were closer, it was easy to see the glass was broken. We found the senior Mr. Flynn on the floor. I didn't feel a strong pulse at first, but he wasn't cold. So, Rob and I started

CPR. When the ambulance took him, his vitals were weak, but he had some."

"Okay. And you mentioned him by name. Did you know the store owner or his son?"

I nodded. "I've been in here a few times. I just brought a watch in for them to fix. I'd appreciate it if you don't mention that in front of Lizzie."

He stopped writing in his notebook. "Why is that?"

"It was my mom's, and I wanted to give it to Lizzie for our birthday."

"And when was that?"

"Actually, earlier this afternoon."

"Did you notice anything odd when you were here? Was there anyone hanging around inside or out that made you suspicious?"

I shook my head. "I was in here alone. I didn't notice anyone else. And I remember the shop was closed when we went to the pub. It was dark inside, and the closed sign was on the door. The father and son were funny together. I could tell there was a lot of respect between them. I hope he's going to be okay. I can't believe someone broke in. Do you think they stole anything?"

"Most break-ins have some sort of theft," he said. "Unless we're looking at assault. How did you see the scene?" He was more curious than suspicious.

"Glass is broken from the outside into the store. Oh. No."

"What?"

"Well, it seems weird for a clock shop to be robbed. Especially in Shamrock Cove. I've been here long enough to know that sort of thing doesn't happen here."

"And?" he asked.

"But they also repair watches and all types of jewelry. Perhaps it was a smash and grab. That's what they call it in the States. And it's terrible to be worried about the watch, but what if it was stolen? I mean, it didn't work, but it was a Rolex. Not that it matters what kind it was. It's that it belonged to my mom."

"Mercy." He put a hand on my shoulder.

"What?"

"Take a breath. In and out slowly."

I did what he asked. "Thanks. Sorry for the ramble. I think I might be in shock. He was so pale, and he'd appeared so hearty earlier today."

"And you didn't see anyone around the store tonight? Any cars parked on the side of the road. That sort of thing."

I took another deep breath. Then I closed my eyes. I blew it out hard. "On the way to the pub there was a black SUV parked outside the shop. I do remember seeing it was dark inside. The shop, not the car."

"Do you know what kind of SUV?"

"I can't tell you the type, but maybe a Land Rover. Or something like that. I'm pretty sure it was black. Though, it could have been a dark blue. The sun was going down when we headed to the pub."

My hands shook a bit. I think the shock might have been catching up with me. I clasped them in front of me.

"Sheila?" She was his second in command.

"Yeah, boss?"

"Is forensics on the way?"

"Two minutes out," she said as she put crime scene tape and some small posts up just outside the door of the store.

"I'm going to walk Ms. McCarthy home. I'll be back in a minute."

"Got it," she said. But I saw her smile.

"You don't have to do that. I'm only a block away."

"Which is why it won't take me long."

When he was like this there was no talking him out of it. We shared the gift of a hard head combined with stubbornness. Sometimes it could be annoying, but I was just as bad.

When I opened the front door, the scent of cookies filled the air.

"Lizzie has been busy," he said.

He was aware my sister baked when she was nervous. It's the only bonus to having a sister who has serious trouble with anxiety. Our mom always said, get out of your head and into your hands. Mom cleared her head by gardening, as did my sister. But Lizzie also loved to bake.

Me, well, I wrote books. Fingers on the keyboard was the one thing that worked to clear my head. I put everything I'd been feeling into my characters and their journeys.

In our kitchen, Scott and Rob sipped tea, while Lizzie took cookies out of the oven. An oven I'd yet to figure out. It was an AGA and on all the time, which with our cool weather was always welcome.

"Mom's chocolate chips?" I asked.

"Yes. I wanted a chocolate fix," she said. "And to keep busy."

"Do you mind if I talk to you quickly?" Kieran asked. "I'll do a more formal interview later."

"That's fine," Scott said. "We are happy to help."

Kieran pulled out his notebook and pen. "Did any of you notice anyone around the store? Inside or out when you arrived."

"No," they said in unison.

"We didn't even notice the broken door until we were closer," Rob said. "Our Mercy is so observant."

The detective inspector grinned. "That she is. What about cars? Maybe, when you were going to the pub?"

Lizzie wiped her hand on a dish towel. "A black Land Rover. I know because I've been looking at them for our road trip."

"Road trip?" he asked.

She glanced at me and then nodded. "To celebrate our

birthday, we decided to go on a road trip through Ireland to get to know it better. But we were going to wait until fall when the summer tourist trade slows down. Which has nothing to do with what happened tonight," she said.

"It's okay," he said calmly. "And you are sure it was black?"

She laughed. "Yes. Because I quite like them, but in all the television shows they belong to some sort of gangster or criminal."

"And football moms," Rob added.

"True," Scott said.

"And when you arrived on the scene tonight, Rob helped with CPR. Who called emergency services?"

"That would be me," Scott said.

"While you were outside, did you notice anyone else?"

"No," We said in unison.

"Right," he said. He snapped his notebook closed. "I need to get back to the scene. If you think of anything else, please let me know."

He turned to leave.

"Wait," Lizzie said. "Take some cookies with you. And do you want some coffee? Mercy can make you one. You may have a long night ahead."

He frowned. "I don't want to trouble you."

We shared a love for coffee. "It's not a problem." I went and made him one in a paper cup, for which we had lids.

Then Lizzie put some cookies in a paper bag.

"Thanks," he said. His cheeks were pink.

"Why don't you walk me out," he said.

I wonder what that is about.

I followed him to our front door.

"What is it?"

"Text me a description of the watch. I'll see if I can find it to put your mind at ease."

"Oh. Uh. Thanks. That is kind. I took a picture of it. I'll text it to you."

"Excellent. See you later."

I was hyped up and there was no way I'd be able to go to sleep any time soon. I very much wanted to find out how poor Mr. Flynn senior was doing.

I headed back to the kitchen.

"I feel bad about sending Mr. Flynn to the hospital alone. I think I'd like to check on him. What if they can't find his son? He'll be alone."

My sister cocked her head and stared at me. "What's going on?"

"What do you mean?" I frowned.

"Do you even know the two Flynns? I mean, they come into the bookstore, but have you met them?"

I shrugged. "I was curious about their clocks and went in the store one day. They have some cool ones. Oh, and remember, I took grandfather's cuckoo to get a once-over when it kept slowing down."

"I don't remember that," she said. "What are you not telling me?"

My sister could always tell when I was hiding something. "It wasn't long after we moved here. Anyway, I don't know them well, but I had met them. He's alone, and elderly. I'm worried about him."

Rob and Scott's heads turned like they were watching a tennis match. This was my sister's gentle way of getting to the truth. She was good at it.

"We all are," she said. "He's a sweet guy. He didn't deserve to get bashed on the head."

"I'll come with you," Rob said. "All that excitement has me on edge."

"I have an early meeting tomorrow. I'm going to finish my cuppa and head home," Scott said.

"Will you be okay alone?" I asked my sister.

"To be honest, I'm exhausted. I thought I'd take Mr. Poe out back and then head up. Make sure you take your key."

"Will do."

I grabbed a scarf, and my mac, because the night was chilly, and Rob and I walked to the hospital, which was only a few blocks away. Everything was close in our wee village, as the people here called it.

Only the emergency doors were open this late. There were a few people sitting in the reception, and a woman at the desk typed on a computer. She held up a finger when we walked up.

We waited patiently.

She handed me a clipboard. "Fill out the paperwork, luv. We're a bit backed up now with an emergency. So, you'll have to wait." She was very Irish and very matter-of-fact.

"I'm not ill. I'm here to check on a patient," I said quickly. I handed her back the clipboard.

"Name?" she asked, but she didn't seem to be very happy with our interruption.

"Flynn," I said.

"And relation?"

"He's her uncle," Rob said.

She stared at her screen. "Right. The doctor will be out to speak to you when he's finished with the patient. Take a seat."

I glanced at Rob. He shrugged. Now, I was embarrassed. What if they needed me to sign some papers or something? Pretending to be a relative could get me in trouble.

"Why did you do that?" I whispered as we sat in the blue plastic chairs.

"She wasn't going to give us anything if we said we were friends. They have to tell the family what is happening. I saw it on the telly."

I laughed. "Not everything on television is real."

"Says you. The fiction writer."

"Exactly," I said.

"We can't leave now," he said. "It will look suspicious. Don't you want to know how he is? I mean, you brought him back to life, Mercy."

"That sounds so dramatic."

"But no less true."

We waited for more than a half-hour, which was just enough time for me to calm down.

"Family for Flynn." A doctor came out. He seemed too young for his field of work, but I wasn't about to say anything.

He took off his hospital cap.

"How is he?" we asked at the same time.

"Not well," the doctor said. "He had a major cardiac infarction, and the head injury is serious. We're going to have to take him to surgery to release pressure off the brain."

"But he'll be okay, right?"

The doctor shook his head. "We're doing everything we can for him. But the next twenty-four hours are critical. I'm sorry. I can't give you false hope. He's in a very serious condition."

"Doctor Mason, code blue. Doctor Mason, code blue."

"Look, I'm sorry it wasn't better news, but I've got to go."

He turned and then ran back through the swinging doors.

"Poor Mr. Flynn," I said. I prayed he made it through the night.

THREE

The next morning, I woke up early. Well, early for me. My sister was already gone, but she'd left me some blueberry muffins. I ate two and shared a bit with Mr. Poe. I needed to write, but I was too curious about the events from the night before. I also wanted to check on Mr. Flynn.

"Let's call it research and head out," I said. "Do you feel like a field trip?"

He cocked his head and stared at me.

"I'm taking that as a yes."

After a quick shower, I checked the weather. We were in for some rain. I pulled on my wellies, and put Mr. Poe's raincoat on him, which also acted as a harness. He didn't mind wet paws but liked the rest of him to stay dry. I didn't blame him. I grabbed my mac and an umbrella. Then I hooked up his leash.

First stop was the police station.

"Hi, Mercy," Sheila said when I came through the door. "And Mr. Poe. Good to see you."

He lifted a paw as if to wave at her.

"He's absolutely brilliant." She laughed.

"He likes to think so," I joked. That said, he was a very bright and intuitive dog.

"Is the detective inspector in?"

"I am," Kieran said from the doorway.

Mr. Poe ran for him. Kieran knelt and gave him a scratch behind the ears. "Hello, little fellow."

"I wondered if I could speak to you about last night," I said.

"By speak to me, do you mean give me the third degree on what we've discovered so far?"

"It's like you know me or something."

Sheila chuckled and Kieran smiled.

"Come on through," he said.

I followed him to his office which was near the back of the small cottage. Like most of the buildings in town, it was several hundred years old and had a thatched roof.

I sat down in the leather chair across from his and Mr. Poe settled with his head on my boots.

"I'm guessing you want to know where we are with the investigation so far?"

"I am. But first have you heard about the elder Mr. Flynn?"

He frowned. "He is in a critical condition. When I checked an hour ago, the doctors said they didn't think he would ever come out of the coma."

My heart dropped. "That is awful. He is so sweet."

"He is."

"Have you found his son?"

"Unfortunately, no. The last anyone saw him—he was headed to Dublin. The police there have been informed and are looking for him."

"Do they have any other family? I don't like the idea of him at the hospital alone."

"His daughter is with him now. It took us a while to get hold of her. She'd been busy cleaning their campsite and left her phone at the house. He's not alone. And I heard there was a niece there last night. Funny, though. He doesn't have a niece." His eyebrows went up.

"Right. In my defense, that was Rob's idea. He said it, and I didn't bother correcting him. We just wanted to know how Mr. Flynn was doing."

"I see."

"You don't, but it wasn't me this time. Have you found out who robbed the store?" I tried to change the subject.

"No. The CCTV isn't very clear because of the rain. It was quick though. No more than five minutes in and out."

"What about the SUV?"

"Nothing there. We checked it out. Belongs to Mac Bannon, but the CCTV shows he was gone before the store was broken into."

"Oh. So, why was Mr. Flynn there?"

"We think he was staying in the apartment above the store. He has a family farm just outside of town, but the daughter said when he's tired, or has a lot of work, he will stay there. He must have heard what was happening and come downstairs."

"But it's a clock store. I mean, he repaired some jewelry. But why break into it? Seems like taking a big chance on not a great pay-off. And I can't imagine fencing a clock is easy."

"I'm still going through the inventory." He picked up a file folder. "I have a list of the logbooks. Your name and the watch are in here."

I closed my eyes and took a deep breath.

"It isn't there," he said. "I'm sorry. It seems to be one of the things that was taken."

For the second time that day, my heart dropped. "Oh. No."

Sensing my distress, Mr. Poe sat up. Then he pawed my leg. He did that often with my sister to comfort her. I picked him up and gave him a squeeze.

"That was the gift for your sister?" he asked.

"Right. But it was my mom's and had a lot of meaning. It's

just a thing and it certainly wasn't worth poor Mr. Flynn's life. I'd been so hopeful that he would be okay."

"The doctors haven't given up, but, like I said, it doesn't look good."

"I need to help. Give me something to do."

"I can't involve you in a police investigation."

I grunted and then rolled my eyes. "Please," I said.

He sighed this time. "Fine. Why don't you try talking to the daughter? When I asked about her brother last night, she shut down. There is something going on with them. Perhaps you can get her to open up. This trip to Dublin is suspicious. At least, the timing is."

"You're wondering if he's skipped town with the goods?"

"You sound like one of your American gangster films. But, yes, it's possible he's done a runner."

"I don't see it," I said.

"Why is that?"

"The father and son had a lovely repartee. It made me think about how Lizzie and I were with our mom. I can't imagine he would hurt his father or steal from their store. It doesn't track. And he would have a key. So, why break in? What if someone has hurt him? Or kidnapped him? I'd believe that before him trying to kill his father."

He shrugged. "Okay. So, you follow up with the daughter. Do that thing where you are able to get people to talk to you."

"You're confusing me with Lizzie, but that gives me an idea."

"Do I want to know?"

"No."

He smirked. "Just don't push too hard or get yourself into trouble."

"Who me?"

He laughed hard.

Mr. Poe stared at him like the detective inspector had gone mad.

"Okay. I'll head up to the hospital. What's the daughter's name?"

"Belinda," he said.

"I'll let you know what I find out."

After waving goodbye to Sheila, we headed down to the bookstore. Mr. Poe was welcome in most places, but the hospital wasn't one of them.

The store had just opened and was empty. When the bell rang over the door, it echoed.

"I'll be there in a minute. Feel free to browse," Lizzie said from her office.

"It's us," I said.

"Oh. Come on back."

I took the leash off Mr. Poe. He had free rein in the store. He ran ahead of me.

"Hello there, handsome," Lizzie said.

By the time I made it to the office, he was already in her arms snuggling against her. Her smile was so peaceful. Every time he did that; it made me love him a little bit more.

"You're up early," she said. "What's going on?"

"I've already been to see Kieran. He asked me to talk to Mr. Flynn's daughter."

Her eyes widened and I laughed.

"Kieran asked for your help?"

"He feels like she might talk to me rather than the police. I told him that wasn't me, that was you."

She smirked. "You want me to use my people skills to find out what?"

I shrugged. "If she knows where her brother is. If there was any bad blood between them. I don't think there was. The father and son were funny together. Like, we used to be with Mom. It felt genuine."

"You seem to like the son," she said. She'd pursed her lips.

"I chatted with him a few times. He was nice, kind even. There was a great respect between the father and son."

"And how did you meet them again?"

"I told you. Our grandfather's clocks. They have some really fun and quirky stuff in there though."

"Do they still think it's a robbery gone wrong?"

I nodded.

"Okay. Well, a few things. Did you eat all the muffins?"

"No," I said.

"Okay, good. We'll have to wait..." The bell rang over the door.

"It's me," Caro said.

"Never mind." After pulling the pencil from behind her ear, Lizzie stood up.

"Caro, Mercy and I need to visit a friend at the hospital. Do you mind watching Mr. Poe for a bit?"

She set him on the floor, and he ran for Caro.

"Oh, look at the cutest dog in the world." She handed him a treat from behind the register. "You two go on. We'll be fine."

We went out the back door.

After a quick stop at home to pick up muffins and a 'get well' card—my sister kept a box of cards for all occasions—we headed to the hospital.

It took us a few minutes, but we found the room. Poor Mr. Flynn was attached to so many tubes and machines, one of which was breathing for him. I didn't know him well, but it hurt my heart to see him like this.

A red-headed woman sat next to the bed holding his hand. She stared at us quizzically when we walked in.

"Do I know you?" she asked. It wasn't a rude question. More out of curiosity.

"Hi, Belinda, we own the bookstore," Lizzie said softly. "You are a big fan of our thriller section. And your dad loves all things history. This is my sister, Mercy, you read her books. She was the one who found your sweet dad last night. We wanted to come check on you. We brought muffins."

She stood. "That's so kind of you," she said. But then she bypassed my sister and went straight for me. She hugged me hard.

I'm not a big hugger, but I squeezed her back.

"Thank you. Who knows what would have happened if you hadn't showed up. I'll never be able to thank you."

"I... No thanks are needed. I quite liked your father. He was very kind to me."

She nodded and dabbed her nose with a tissue. "Never met a stranger, my da. But thank you again. She's right, I do read your books. I love them."

"Uh. Thanks." I never knew how to take praise.

"How is he?" Lizzie asked softly. She set the basket of muffins on a shelf.

"It isn't good. The doctors just came in and said there has been no improvement. I can't believe this. I've been praying for a miracle."

"It's awful, you poor thing," Lizzie said. "And you're alone. Where is Declan?"

"I've been calling my brother over and over, but he's not answering," she said. "I'm so worried about him. The police think he went off to Dublin, but on a Thursday. I could see for the weekend. He has a woman he's been seeing, but I don't know if she lives there. What if whoever did this to my father also hurt my brother?"

"That is scary to think," I said. "But the police will be checking CCTV for the Dublin trains, so hopefully they will be able to put your mind at rest."

"That would be grand. I've been thinking the worst. It isn't like him not to tell me if he's leaving. I take care of things at the farm. He and Da handle the store. That's the way it has always been. Never been robbed. In all the years Da had the shop. I just don't understand it."

My sister guided Belinda back to her chair, and then she sat in the one on the other side of the bed. That left the window ledge for me.

"It's a terrible thing," Lizzie said. "I can't imagine what you're going through right now. Is there anything we can do to locate your brother? Any other places he might go? Maybe he has a hobby like fishing? Could he be off doing that?"

I gave Lizzie a look and crossed my eyes.

She ignored me.

"He likes anything outdoors. To be honest, I always thought it strange Da gave the farm to me. But Declan loves working on clocks. Like our da, he has a bit of the engineer in him. Always pulling things apart and putting them back together. I wish he were here. I can't make these decisions about Da alone." She sniffled.

This was all too reminiscent of those last days with my mom. I hadn't thought about that until we entered the room. It was the smell of hospitals. Mom hated them as well. We ended up doing hospice at home and she left peacefully, devastating those left behind. My sister and I were better than we had been, but grief was a slow process. I wasn't sure that the hole Mom left would ever be filled.

We understood how Belinda felt more than most. Though, luckily for us, my mom made her final decisions. We didn't have to make the hard choices. Mom was brilliant to the end.

"I shouldn't say this, but we are rather good at snooping," Lizzie said. "We've helped the police a few times with their cases. And it sounds like you need help."

"Will you, really?"

"Of course," I said. "Tell us what you need."

"Could you check the farm? We keep a few glamping sites and spaces for caravans. It could be Declan's holed up in one of those. Sometimes he'd take a few days off from the store and hang out there. At night, we have great stargazing. I keep calling him, but it's possible he left his phone at the shop or at the farm and I didn't notice. Or he's being an eejit and turned it off. He's famous for that when he wants some peace and quiet."

"We can go check the farm for you," I said. "That's no problem at all."

"I... feel bad asking for help, but I don't have anyone else," she said. "Da and my brother are my world."

"You are not alone," Lizzie said. She reached across the bed and squeezed her hand. "We are here for you. Mercy is going to write down our numbers. I'll come by tonight to stay with your father so you can take a bit of a break. At least, grab a shower and change of clothes. And I'll have some lunch sent to you. I don't know about the food here, but hospital dining can get old quickly."

"I don't know what to say."

"You don't have to say anything. Also, I'm going to sign up some of my friends to help you out, if you're okay with that. They are all our very best friends, and I know they would love to help."

"You're too kind. Oh, I nearly forgot. Joseph should be back today. He's been in Kenmare at an auction. He is the manager of the farm. If you run into him, tell him I sent you. I texted but I have no idea if he got the message."

"Give Mercy your phone. She'll put our numbers in," Lizzie said.

Belinda pulled her phone out of her bag. "Thank you. You're so kind."

"Lizzie loves taking care of people, and she's right. We have the most amazing friends. They will be happy to help out. Like she said, you're not alone."

Lizzie kept her busy while I put our numbers in her phone. Then I quickly checked her call log and messages. There was nothing suspect. But she did have a number for her brother, which she had called and texted many times.

I quickly put the number in my phone.

"We'll go check the farm for you, but I'm texting my friend Rob," Lizzie said. "He's a wonderful chef, and he'll bring you some lunch."

"Wait. You're friends with Food Truck Rob?"

I had to hold back a laugh.

"We are," Lizzie said. "He's off today. And he always loves cooking for people. Do you have something you want?"

"I love his Thai sandwiches."

Lizzie went around the bed and hugged her. "We do too. Though, I've never eaten anything I didn't love from him. Please, know you are not alone. We'll find your brother. And you will be surrounded by friends. Everyone loved your father. We want to be here for him."

Belinda cleared her throat. "Thank you. You two are a blessing."

They squeezed each other. I sometimes wished I was more like Lizzie. She had an innate way of knowing what people needed at any given moment.

"Do we need to do anything while we are out there?" I asked. "Do we need to feed the animals or something since it is a farm?"

"No. I did it before I came in this morning and Joseph should be there soon. He was due back before lunch. I'll text him again and let him know you're coming. Not that he'll read it. He's as bad as my brother."

"Thanks," I said. "I hate to ask this, but is there anyone you know who might want to cause your family harm?"

She sighed.

"You can tell us anything," Lizzie said.

"We've been at odds with the farm next door," she said. "The Donnels and my family have a long and disturbing history. But I can't imagine them hurting Da. They might steal some sheep or a cow, but this is too far, even for them."

From what I'd heard about them, maybe not. They were worth checking into, at least.

"And there's Mr. Simmons, he owns the jewelry store in town. He and Da were always at it. Mostly shouting at each other. I can't imagine him hurting Da, though."

When people were pushed too far, though, they sometimes did awful things.

"We'll be back later to visit, but call if you need anything and don't be shy about it," Lizzie said.

Belinda smiled and then nodded.

We headed out.

"You are really good at that."

"What? Asking questions without seeming like that is what I'm doing and giving you a chance to copy numbers off her phone?"

It was eerie how our minds sometimes became one. That was just one of the many benefits of being a twin.

"That and the way you make people feel loved and cared for at any given moment. It is a gift."

She sighed as we walked outside. "It wasn't that long ago that we experienced loss, and we felt so alone. At least, we had each other."

Darn I was mad at myself for reminding her.

Not long after we lost our mom, Lizzie's fiancé and his daughter were killed in a terrible car accident. It was one of the main reasons we'd picked up our broken lives and moved to Ireland. The other being we were contacted by our grandfather's lawyer about inheriting his home and store. A grandfather we'd never known about since he was my dad's father. We'd never known our father.

Though, there had been a moment a few months ago when we thought he may have been hospitalized in our small town. But by the time we heard about it, the man had disappeared.

"I'm nervous about going out to the farm," she said. "The last time we did something like this we found a dead man." She shivered.

"You don't have to come with me," I said. "That isn't a guilt trip. The last thing I want is for you to be upset about anything. I will not add to your anxiety."

"I'll be more anxious if you go out there alone. Let's get Mr. Poe, though. I always feel safer when he's around."

I smiled. He might lick someone to death, but there wasn't much Mr. Poe could do if we found ourselves in trouble.

Though, he was rather good at finding dead bodies.

FOUR

After a quick stop by the house—where my sister had managed
to put together some sandwiches for us to eat in the car, along
with a Thermos of coffee—we were on our way. Mr. Poe was
the beneficiary of my crusts, which always annoyed my sister.
He sat between us in his special car seat.

"That isn't healthy for him," she chastised. "The vet said we
have to watch his weight."

"You look at those eyes and tell me how you avoid giving
him whatever he wants."

"Mr. Poe, you need to stop snacking," she said. He turned
and cocked his head. She sighed. "You might be right about
that. But no, I'm not feeding you."

He quickly turned back to me, and we laughed.

"Is it sad that I'm sitting here begging the universe that we
don't find a dead body?" she asked.

"Given what has happened in the past, you have every
right. I just feel like to ease Belinda's mind, we need to check in
and make sure everything is okay. Maybe we'll get lucky and
find her brother."

"Alive. Let's be specific about that."

"Yes. What you said."

After driving down a long dirt road, which was extremely muddy from the rain, we made it to the gate.

"I'll get it," she said before I could get out of the car. We'd both worn our wellies since we were headed to a farm. She opened the metal gate, and I drove over the cattle guard. Well, that's what we called them in Texas. Here in Ireland, the guard was probably more for sheep than cattle.

We followed the dirt road to a thatched cottage which rambled to the right and left as if it had been built onto throughout the years. It was painted white with a dark-green trim. It looked like something out of a storybook for children.

"It's so pretty," Lizzie said.

"Yes, it is. She said it should be unlocked." People here in Shamrock Cove never locked their doors. But Lizzie and I did. After living in Manhattan for a few decades it was habit. And I'd had stalkers. We were both overly conscious where security was concerned.

I knocked first. It didn't seem right to burst straight in. We had no idea if Declan was aware of what had happened to his dad. If he'd left his phone at home and gone out into nature, who knew?

We waited, but no one answered. I opened the door slowly.

"Hello? Is anyone home? I'm Mercy, and I'm here with my sister Lizzie."

An eerie silence followed.

"I don't think anyone is here," she whispered.

I smiled. "I agree. But let's check the rooms to make certain."

"Please, do not suggest we split up," she said.

"I wouldn't dare."

She had Mr. Poe on his leash. "Wipe your feet," she said to him.

He did what she asked. He really was quite brilliant.

We headed to the kitchen first. It was to the right when we walked inside the home. Everything was incredibly neat and organized. There were no dishes in the sink, and the place smelled of lemons.

On the other side of the entry was the living area. The furniture was well-worn, but neat and not a spot of dust anywhere. There was a boho-chic vibe happening that made everything feel cozy. There was a door off the living room, and we opened it.

"I'm guessing this is the elder Mr. Flynn's room since it is on the first floor." There were some photos on the dresser of a woman in the sixties. She was quite beautiful even though her hair was what we Texans would call a beehive. In the closet were clothes an older man would wear. Again, everything was incredibly neat. It didn't feel right going through the man's dresser, though I very much wanted to. But that wouldn't help us find Declan.

Upstairs, there were two bedrooms off a hallway. One belonged to a woman, which was evident when we walked inside. The room smelled of vanilla and there was flowered wallpaper that matched the bedspread.

"Please, don't riffle through her things," my sister said.

I smiled. "I wasn't going to, but I will in the brother's room."

She sighed.

The other room was stark. Nothing on the walls. Just a bed, dresser, and a nightstand.

"You stand at the door. If he does come home, I don't want him to find me going through his things."

She grunted. "I don't like this part."

"But we need to find him. We promised her."

"Fine," Lizzie said. "Come on, Mr. Poe. We're standing guard." They turned away from me. I went through the drawers in the dressers. I was careful and put everything back where I'd found it. I didn't find any secret notebooks or hints that the brother might have some sort of gambling problem, which was where my mind had gone.

Nor did I find any pictures of a woman. If he was serious about the woman in Dublin, it felt like he should have had something of hers. The closet was tiny, and the plaid shirts and cable-knit sweaters were stuffed into it. There was a box on the top shelf. I had to stand on my toes to reach it.

I pulled it down and set it on the bed. When I opened the lid, I frowned. "Interesting."

She turned back. "What did you find?" she asked.

"A box of odds and ends, but it is weird that he has photos of several of the clocks in the store. I remember seeing these. But the one with the eagle on the top was missing that night when I glanced around."

"How can you even remember that? Maybe they sold it. How long ago were you in there?"

I shrugged. No way I would say because she might suspect my reason for being in there. Kieran hadn't found the watch yet, but I prayed it was just hidden in a safe somewhere. "I had noticed it when I'd been in before. I wonder if it's worth a lot."

I took photos of all the pictures with my phone. If nothing else, they were something Kieran should check out. Especially if some of the items had been stolen.

Was this possibly an insurance scam? It wouldn't be the first time a store owner had pulled something like that. Keeping a business going in today's economy was rough. Not that it excused that sort of behavior.

There was a rosary, as well. I took a picture of that. Then I put the lid back on the box and returned it to where I had found it in the closet.

"What are you taking pictures of in that box?" Lizzie glanced back at me.

"Photos of things that might have been in the store." I told her about the possible insurance scam.

"But then where would they hide the items? And why hurt poor Mr. Flynn if they pulled the job themselves?"

"Very good questions. It just seems weird they would have pictures of the items in their store."

"Could be his way of keeping inventory. Not everyone is as careful as I am about keeping the books."

"True."

I peeked under the bed but only found some storage boxes with clothing.

My sister's phone dinged, and we both jumped. She pulled her phone from her pocket. "Oh, good," she said.

"What is it?"

"Rob is at the hospital with Belinda. He took her lunch. And our friends have set up a schedule, so she isn't alone. They are the best."

"Yes, they are."

Her phone dinged again. She smiled. "And Lolly says she has dinner sorted. Belinda is not going hungry while she's there. I really hope a miracle happens and Mr. Flynn wakes up. It's so sad. And so obvious how much she loves her dad."

"It is sad. I'm glad we can all be there for her."

"What if something has happened to her brother? That is a lot of loss."

She was thinking about her past experiences.

"Don't borrow trouble, as Mom used to say. Let's stay positive."

She nodded.

We headed downstairs. There was only one room we hadn't checked on and that was at the back of the house, what they called a snug here. There was a television on the wall and an L-shaped comfy couch, along with a couple of recliners. There was a bookshelf on the far wall.

We walked over to read some of the titles.

Lizzie smiled. "They bought a lot of these in the shop."

"Do you remember everything people purchase?"

"I think we have my OCD to thank for that. I don't know why I do, but it happens. Helps when clients can't remember if they've already bought something. And when it comes to doing that inventory."

My sister had a head for all kinds of math.

I did not.

I was a writer, but math had never been fun for me.

There was a sound outside, and I stopped. "Did you hear that?"

"No," she said. Mr. Poe barked. "But he did."

I motioned for her to follow me. I carefully opened the front door and gasped.

My sister screamed behind me, and Mr. Poe rushed forward.

FIVE

"Who are you and what are you doing in the Flynns' house," a man yelled as he pointed a rifle at us. My hands went up in surrender. "You must be Joseph," I said quickly. "Belinda sent us out to check on things. She was hoping we might be able to find her brother. We promised we would take a look."

"My sister writes detective stories, but she's also really good at finding people," Lizzie said quickly behind me.

She left out the part where they were usually dead by the time I found them.

Mr. Poe growled. He had put himself between us and the gunman. He really was a very brave boy.

"Could you please put the rifle down?" I asked.

He glanced at it, as if he'd forgotten. Then he lowered it to his side. "Sorry about that. Can't be too careful out here. Everyone knows our Flynn is in the hospital and that his daughter is there. I just came back from an auction to the news. When I saw the car, I thought the worst."

"That's understandable," I said. "Do you have any idea where Declan might be? We were hoping we might run into him out here. Belinda is desperate to find him."

He smirked. "Probably off on one of his benders in the city."

"Oh? His sister said he liked the outdoors and that he might be at one of the glamping sites." She didn't mention he had a drinking problem.

He shrugged. "He does that sometimes. Never fond of too much responsibility, that one. But he also goes on benders, something she isn't likely to mention. She loves her brother and only wants to see the good in people."

I had a feeling Joseph didn't have the same attitude toward Declan.

"You don't think he could hurt his dad, do you?" my sister asked from behind me.

"No," he said. "They are a close family and love one another. That I can say. He would never do anything to hurt his da. I could have checked on things, why didn't Belinda call me?"

"She said she did," I said.

He checked his pockets. "Ah. Left my phone in the lorry."

"Do you live in one of the glamping sites?"

"No. My caravan is on the other side of the property. I like staying close to the animals. The barns are there and the grazing fields."

"She said you would be taking care of the animals."

"That's my job," he said proudly. "And I'll be keeping an eye on the place. Please tell her that. She's not to worry."

"We will," Lizzie said.

"Do you mind if we check out the glamping sites? Just to make sure he isn't in one of them?"

"I could check, but feel free. Whatever sets her mind at ease works for me. Do you need keys?"

I held up the key fob Belinda had given us. "We're good."

"Follow the road around the house. Sites are past the hill."

"I nearly peed my pants," my sister whispered when Joseph drove off in his truck—or lorry, as they called them here.

"Right there with you, sister. I'm never fond of guns."

"Even though you use them a lot in your books."

I sighed. "True." We closed up the house and climbed into our SUV.

"My heart is still beating too fast," she said. Mr. Poe grunted as if he agreed.

"That was a little scary."

"A little?"

"Okay, a lot." I had to engage the four-by-four to get up the hill, but it was worth it. On the other side was a lush valley with several yurts. But they were made with clear tops for stargazing.

"Those are really cool," she said.

Fairy lights had been strung up on poles surrounding the grounds, and there was a gigantic fire pit in the center with stone seats all around.

"I agree. It would be fun to come out and watch the stars."

We stopped at the first one. It was unlocked, so I didn't need the key. But stopped myself, and knocked first. "Is anyone there?" I called out.

No one answered.

We went inside. There was a bed, nightstands, lamps and a few chairs. Everything was decorated in bright colors and very boho chic. It was definitely my sister's style.

"I wonder if Belinda decorated these," I said.

"It's a lot like her taste in the house, so I expect she did. I love her style."

There was a small kitchenette to the right and a tiny bathroom on the other side. But glancing up was what mattered. We watched the clouds stroll by.

"Definitely cool," my sister said.

"It is. And we wouldn't have to share a bathroom with other people." That, and insects, were my main complaints for experiencing the great outdoors. This would exclude both of those things. I could get into this kind of camping, or glamping.

We laughed. We were not people who particularly liked living rough. I'd worked too hard for too long to go without a private bath. Did that make me a snob? Maybe. But I was okay with it.

Lizzie felt the same way.

We went through each of the yurts quickly. And didn't find anything. Until the last one. For some reason, it was locked.

"That's weird," I said.

"Maybe it just caught when they walked out. Like our back door does sometimes."

"Could be." I went through a few of the keys and eventually found the right one.

"Do you think the neighbors are as bad as they say? Those Donnels?"

"You saw them the other night at the pub. They were loud, but we can't judge by that. Though, remember Lolly wasn't a fan."

"True. And like Mr. Poe, she's a great judge of character."

I pushed down on the handle and opened the door. As I had with each little home, I called out. "Hello? Anyone here?"

No one answered.

When we entered, this one was messy. Someone had slept in the bed and hadn't bothered making it up. My sister headed toward the kitchen area to check the small fridge.

I headed to the bathroom. At first, everything appeared to be clean, but then I noticed some reddish-brown spots in the drain.

Is that blood?

I pulled my magnifying glass out of my backpack. On the back side of the faucet, was a bloody fingerprint.

But whose?

Had Declan been staying out here? And why would he be bloody?

Everyone we'd talked to said there was no way he would ever harm his father.

But in the heat of a crime, things could happen. Perhaps it had been an accident.

Why though? The motive was really messing me up. He certainly had a key to the shop, so why break into it? And he probably could have snuck stolen items out without anyone knowing.

"Why are you staring at the bathroom?" my sister whispered beside me.

I jumped. I'd been so involved in my thoughts, that I hadn't heard her walk up.

Mr. Poe sniffed the air and then barked.

"Mr. Poe says something is wrong," she said. "What is it?"

"I need to call Kieran."

"Oh, this can't be good."

It wasn't.

We sat in the car for about a half-hour before Kieran and his team arrived. We didn't want to risk messing up anything else with the scene.

"And you were out here, why?" Kieran asked me questions through the driver-side window. It was obvious he wasn't happy with me.

"We had permission," my sister said quickly. "We promised Belinda we would check to see if we could find Declan Flynn."

"And you found the bathroom a mess, so you called me?"

I nodded. "Right. It might have been left over from a previous camper," I said.

He smirked. "And the bed was messed up?"

"Yes. The others were neat and tidy."

"We also checked the house," Lizzie said. "If you find our fingerprints there, that is why. Again, we had permission."

Kieran covered his mouth with a cough. It was obvious he was trying to hide a smile. My sister was nervous and tended to overcompensate when she had any sense of guilt.

"Right. But why wouldn't he stay at his own home? Why out here?" he asked.

"Maybe so he wouldn't be seen," I said. "Again, we have no way of knowing if it was him. But his sister doesn't seem the type to leave one of the yurts dirty."

"Okay. And you haven't seen anyone else?"

I told him about Joseph.

"I know him from the pub. Does he live on the property?"

"Yes. He said he had a caravan near the barns. He looks after the animals."

"He showed up at the front door with a gun and scared the pants off us," Lizzie babbled. Kieran made her nervous when he was investigating.

"A gun?" he asked curiously.

"He thought we were intruders. He didn't try to shoot us."

"At least there is that." He sighed.

I smiled. That was a phrase he'd picked up from me.

"Did you touch anything else?"

My sister grunted.

Kieran gave me the eye.

"There was a box in the brother's closet. I may have taken pictures. I'm fairly certain I remember seeing some of the items in the shop. Might be his way of keeping inventory or something."

"Okay. Send me the pictures, though we'll probably take the box into evidence. I need a warrant for the house first. That could take a day or so."

"I'll send them to you," I said.

"Anything else you need to tell me?"

"The Donnels are not friends," Lizzie said quickly. I gave her a look and she shrugged. "He needs to know."

"I've come out here a few times for their feud. It's ongoing," he said. "And I have had various family members in residence at the station."

I nodded. "Your grandmother hinted about the same."

"If that's it, you two are good to go home. Please stay out of trouble."

"We'll try," I said.

He laughed as he walked away.

"I feel as though we are like a never-ending source of amusement for him," Lizzie said.

"And frustration."

"True."

We headed home.

"Can you drop me at the store? I feel bad that Caro has been handling everything. I'll take Mr. Poe. He's due a good walk this evening."

Mr. Poe grunted.

After dropping them off, and parking on Main Street. I headed around the corner to our home.

So many facts rolled through my brain, and I needed to sit down and write them in my notebook.

After hanging up my backpack, there was noise in the back of the house.

I picked up one of the umbrellas from our stand.

"Who's there? I have a weapon."

Once again, I was met with an eerie silence.

Crud.

This sort of thing never went well for me.

SIX

There was a note on the floor by the back door, as if someone had shoved it underneath. I tried the door, and it was unlocked. The alarm should have been going off. *That's weird.* Unless one of us had forgotten to set it. I'd only been half awake when I'd left earlier. I didn't remember checking the door or the alarm. It was probably my fault.

I ran out and into the backyard. No one was there. A big gust of wind blew so hard, it nearly knocked me down. I glanced back at the door.

I let the breath I'd been holding out.

"I'm being paranoid." Though, my questioning everything had saved my life more than once.

I headed back inside and was about to put the umbrella away when I picked up the piece of paper from the floor.

It was a hastily scrawled note.

Please help me. I know you've done it for others. I didn't hurt my da. I was at the Raven's Pub in Dublin last night. But I know who.

That was it. The note wasn't finished or signed. But there was a drop of blood on it.

"Mercy, are you okay?" my sister called out.

Before I could answer, Mr. Poe ran past and scratched on the door.

"I'm here. Don't come in, though. I need to call Kieran."

"Why is that?" she asked worriedly from the hallway. She peeked into the kitchen. She held up an umbrella. That was our weapon of choice.

"Someone has been here. I don't want to mess up a crime scene if that is what is going on. Why are you here? I just left you."

"I had one of our weird twin moments that made me panic. I tried to call you, but when you didn't answer I was worried."

"Sorry. My phone is in my backpack hanging by the door. Can you do me a favor and call Kieran. Tell him there is blood on a note in our kitchen."

"Blood?" The word came out on a whisper. The kitchen was her favorite room in our house, and it was meticulously clean.

"Yes, but just on the note. They never came inside. I think from Declan, though it isn't signed so I can't be sure. He says he didn't hurt his dad."

"Why would he be here?"

"I think he was trying to ask us for help. Maybe he spoke to Belinda."

Mr. Poe scratched the door and whined.

"He really needs to go out," she said.

"Hopefully, he doesn't disturb any more than he already has." I let him out and the door swung open. He rushed to the back gate and had a fit. He tried to jump over the gate. His bark was sharp and kind of scary.

"Stay here, and call Kieran. I need to see why Mr. Poe is so upset."

"Mercy, what if the bad guy is out there? Please wait for the police."

"And leave Mr. Poe alone?"

I grabbed my trusty umbrella again and headed out. Mr. Poe was going insane.

"Is something wrong over there?" Rob called out from his back porch. "Mr. Poe sounds like he is upset."

"We have a situation," I said. "Someone left us a note under the door. I think he's trying to follow their tracks."

"I'm coming over."

I didn't bother to say he didn't have to help. Rob was sensible and great in a crisis.

When I reached the gate, I picked up Mr. Poe. I didn't want him to run out. But when I went through, my breath caught in my throat.

Declan was face down on the ground.

"Oh. No," Rob said from behind me.

"Hold him." I handed him Mr. Poe, who had finally quieted down. I went to check for a pulse. There wasn't one. Blood pooled on the back of his head. It appeared he'd been hit with something large. But a lot of it was already dried. Had someone hit him before he arrived? I felt bad for the poor man. He'd come to us for help. His hand was crudely bandaged, but the blood on that was dried.

Maybe he had been in the yurt. Kieran would know if the blood matched. But why was he dead? The wound on his head appeared mostly dried. None of this made sense.

I glanced up at Rob. He was already on his phone calling for an ambulance. But I didn't think there was any hope. Poor Declan was quite cold and had been lying there for a bit.

"That's the guy from the clock shop," Rob said, after hanging up his phone.

"It is the son. That poor family."

"Why is he here behind your gate?"

"I think he wanted us to help him prove he didn't hurt his dad. There was a note under our kitchen door, but he didn't finish it. Maybe whoever is after him showed up, and he ran out."

Blood seeped into the grass on the back path. "He has a nasty head wound."

"That means the killer was near your house. He might know who you are."

I sighed. "Shhh. Please don't say that when my sister is around. I don't want her to worry. It looks like he might have been followed here and then chased. But I'm no forensic expert."

"But I am," Kieran said from the other side of the gate. "Are you okay?"

I nodded.

He knelt and searched for a pulse on the dead man.

"Tell me everything," he said.

So, I did.

A few hours later, my sister and I went with Kieran to the hospital. We didn't want Declan's sister, Belinda, to hear the news alone. In the last twenty-four hours, her brother had been murdered, and her poor dad was still in critical care. Lizzie and I understood that overwhelming sense of loss and it had been my sister's idea to come here and be with her.

When we arrived with Kieran, she glanced up, and it was if she knew. "No. Not Declan. Please."

Kieran headed in and we followed.

"I'm sorry," he said. "We found your brother on the back path behind the court."

She sobbed. "He called me a few hours ago. Said he was back and stayed in one of the yurts. Said he'd cut his hand on a knife, but he was okay. He claimed someone was following him.

I thought he was being paranoid. I told him to go to the police, but he swore you would never believe him."

"Did he mention who was after him?"

"No. Said it was safer if I didn't know anything. But I don't understand. I can't believe he wouldn't stop and see me and Da."

"Did you mention we were helping you?" I asked.

She nodded. "I told him we could trust you. I looked you up on the internet. You've helped on several cases."

Much to Kieran's chagrin, but my being a mystery writer made a fun tie-in for the local newspaper.

"I explained that you'd been trying to find him for me. I said you'd helped solve other cases for people. No offense, Detective Inspector."

"None taken. You aren't wrong."

That might have been the nicest thing he ever said about me. Though, I was fairly certain he was offended. Kieran was a straight arrow and quite dedicated to the residents of Shamrock Cove. He would do anything to keep them safe. Now, he had an attack and a murder to solve.

"I know Kieran asked this before, and so did we, but is there anyone who might want to hurt your family or Declan?"

She shook her head.

"Think carefully," Lizzie said. "Has anyone made threats to the family or your farm? Other than the Donnels. Maybe you have a glamping client who wasn't happy? Something like that."

Belinda sobbed. "I wish I could think of someone." She blew her nose. "We do sometimes get complaints. The water isn't always hot in the showers, or an animal finds its way into one of the yurts, but nothing major. It's mostly the Donnels who complain."

"Anything recent?" Kieran asked.

"They weren't happy about our yurts. Said they were a blight on the scenery. And our clients sometimes trespass onto their land. We try to make it clear by marking things off with posts and flags, but some people don't listen. Seamus Donnel and my brother kicked off not long ago about something. I can't tell you what it was about though."

"Right. I'll check into that," Kieran said. "Anyone else?"

"Last week Da was upset with some guy wanting to buy the building from him. The one the shop is in. Max or Mac? I can't remember. My brother told me that he kicked the guy out and threatened he'd sell over his dead body. The building has been in our family for hundreds of years. The farm has always been a hobby for Da. His clocks were his babies."

She smiled through her tears. "He loves us dearly. But he can get lost in fixing things. He loves the precision of watches and the mechanics. Poor Declan was just like him.

"Oh, Da, you have to wake up. I need you to be okay." She sobbed. And my sister wrapped her arms around her. I had to turn away before I lost it as well.

Kieran walked out and I followed him.

"That is two solid leads," I said.

"It is. But I don't have a name for the man she mentioned, who wanted to buy the property."

"Yes, you do," I said. "And I'll tell you if you let me help."

"You want to go and interview these people with me, don't you?"

I smiled. "You know you could make me an official consultant. You know I can be helpful."

He sighed. "I'm only saying do not go off on your own, as you might find yourself in trouble."

"It's like you know me." I smiled.

He didn't do it, but I was fairly certain he wanted to roll his eyes.

"If you tag along, you have to promise to let me ask the questions." He gave me that stare. The one that said he wasn't putting up with any shenanigans.

But I liked shenanigans. Sometimes that was the only way to get people to be honest.

I crossed my heart.

He sighed. "I don't believe you."

I grinned. He really was a very bright man. But with the summer fête and tourism on the line, we had to find the killer. The last thing the town needed was the media talking about break-ins and murder.

SEVEN

The next day, I met Kieran outside the clock shop. It was early for me. Around seven. We had several people to talk to today, and the detective inspector wanted to start by searching the shop again.

"Remind me why we are here?"

"My team is going through CCTV to find the guy Belinda mentioned, but we don't have a name. And I'm hoping we can find some kind of business card."

"Do people even use those anymore?"

He chuckled. "Not all of us are as fond of gadgets as you are. Many people still depend on paper."

I held up my hands in surrender. "Hey, books also come in paper. I'm a great lover of the real thing."

"I bet you are."

"Anyway, I think your culprit is Mac Bannon. Remember, his SUV was parked in front of the store before the break-in."

Kieran snapped his fingers. "You're right. He is a property developer. That must be who Belinda spoke about. I'll check in with him again. Though, I did follow up on his alibi. He was in Dublin at the time of the break-in."

"It would be so much easier to solve if the big bad property developer turned out to be both the thief and the murderer."

"True. Though he comes with a group of solicitors."

"That's no fun. But in books and television shows, the property developer often has henchmen. Perhaps one of them could have broken in."

He grunted. "I think that's a bit of a reach, but I'll keep it in mind."

He used a key to open the boarded-up door. The glass had been cleaned off the floor. Some of the clocks were a bit wayward on the walls. I moved to straighten them and then stopped.

"It's okay. Everything has been dusted, and we have pictures," he said. "I'm going to check in the back. Why don't you take a look at his workbench? Look for anything that might seem out of order. Papers and such."

"I know he has an alibi, but what if the property developer was after more than one building? My guess is he has asked some of the other shop owners if they might be interested in selling. Someone like that would possibly be looking at buying up a block or something."

"You're not going to let this go, are you?"

I scrunched up my face. "I still think powerful guys like that have someone else to do their dirty work."

He nodded. "Okay. I'll check into it."

"I'm curious why we are here," I said. "Isn't this something you would normally relegate to someone on your team?"

He nodded. "True, but as of last night more than three-fourths of my staff is out with a late flu. It was going around the schools, and now it's hit our team. I'll be running point on most everything with this case."

"I see." That was probably why he hadn't fought much with me helping. While he was often frustrated with me, I was helpful.

After straightening the clocks on the walls, I went to investigate. Everything had been put away neatly. No tools were out of place. Well, at least as far as I could tell. The elder Mr. Flynn was fastidious. There was a drawer with files at the bottom, and I carefully went through them. I didn't find anything that looked suspicious. Though, I'm not certain I would have known if I'd run across it. There were client invoices, and some receipts for parts. But not much else.

"I'm coming up with nothing out here. How about you?" I walked into the back room where he sat at a desk. There were several more files, and he was carefully going through each one.

"Still looking. Any chance you want to check the safe?"

"I thought it was empty?" Which had been very disappointing to me.

"There's another one." He pointed to the back wall. "Belinda says it's behind the cuckoo. Here's the combination." He handed me a piece of paper.

"Don't you need to dust it for fingerprints?"

"We have yours on file," he said. "Besides, you're wearing gloves."

"But what if I smudge the criminal's prints?"

"We dusted the clock. Only found the elder Mr. Flynn's. Killer would have had to move the clock to find the safe."

That made sense. If I were police, I'd check everything. Though, I had no reason to doubt Kieran's abilities. He'd worked as an officer all over Ireland and the UK and was quite good at his job.

I carefully moved the clock. There were some books behind it, and I shifted those as well. Sure enough, there was a small safe built into the wall.

Please, be some sort of clue. And, please, let Mom's watch be in here.

I used the code. It took me two tries, but it finally popped open. There were passports, and some legal papers. But no jewelry.

Bummer. I'd been praying the watch was in there. It wasn't so much that I would now have to find another gift for my sister, it was far more that I'd lost a precious item that belonged to our mom. One of the few things I'd found that might have belonged to our father. Not that I had any proof of that.

"Anything?" he asked.

I held up the passports. "Odd that they would keep them here and not at home, right?" I asked.

"Could be they don't have a safe at home and thought this was the best place to keep them."

"You may be right."

"Anything else?"

"I did find the deed to the building. It is in the elder Mr. Flynn's name, which isn't surprising. There is also a will. Can I open it?"

"We found it in due course, so go ahead."

I brought it over to the desk and unfolded it. Belinda received the farm and home, and Declan inherited the business and a boat. Unless something happened to one of them. Then everything would go to the remaining sibling. I hadn't heard about the boat before.

"Maybe we should check the boat," I said.

"You think Declan may have been hiding out there?"

I nodded. "Well, we know he was at the yurt at some point, but you would know better than me. Since you did forensics on the glamping site yesterday. But it's possible he was moving between the two. You can get to the harbor from their farm if you take the long road around. Or he could have been..."

"What?" he asked.

"Using the path that runs from the castle's parking lot down to the shore. It's the track behind the court. But it would be the perfect way to come and go without being seen. Perhaps that's how he ended up behind our house."

He nodded.

"We accidentally took that route, the long way around, when we left the other day. I turned left instead of right, and we drove across the cliffs. But it would be quite a hike. I mean, it's not so far from the castle, but from their farm, probably four or five miles."

"Maybe he had transportation we haven't found yet," Kieran offered.

"You're right. Any luck with those files?" I asked.

"I did find the inventory. I'm taking it back to the office. I'll have the team compare it to the photos of inventory we found. And he's logged your watch. So, it's recent."

I blew out a breath. "I'm curious about what exactly was stolen."

"I am as well. I've noticed a lot of books back here. I thought they might be manuals on fixing things. Some of them are. But others are fiction and appear quite old. Do you mind checking through them?"

"Me, looking at books? Yep, not a problem."

He laughed. "I really appreciate your help. The town council is on me to find the killer or killers quickly and put all this to bed. It isn't good for the town having killers running around."

"I have to agree with them, as this is supposed to be one of the safest places to live and visit. But I will help in any way I can."

I started at the far end. Many of the books were manuals, as he said. Some were to fix very old clocks and were fascinating. But mixed in were several first editions. Many of which would bring in some good cash. His library wasn't as good as the ones in our grandfather's home library, but it was close.

"He has a first edition James Joyce," I whispered.

"Is that worth a great deal?" Kieran asked.

"I'm not a book dealer, but I would assume so. I would keep something like this hidden away. Anyone could pick it up."

"Maybe he didn't know how much it was worth. Lot of things are passed down in families around here. Unlike you Yanks, we don't always go for the newest items."

I smiled. "Hey, except for the television over the fireplace in my office we haven't changed much of anything in Grandad's place. Well, we added some of our art. But as far as furniture goes, we've kept it all."

Our grandfather had amazing taste. His home and bookstore were fairy-tale places for us.

"Are you ready to head upstairs?" he asked. Just as he said the words his phone rang.

"Sergeant, what's that?" He frowned. "I'll be there in ten."

He ended the call.

"I need to run this logbook and the other items back to the station. And they need me there for a... situation. I wonder if you could do me a favor?"

"Sure. What do you need?"

"When I questioned Belinda last night about her brother, she clammed up. I think she knows more than she's saying."

"Oh?" I was surprised by this turn of events. "What do you want me to ask?"

"About the boat. And him hiding. What did he say to her when they spoke? Maybe emphasize that we really need to know in order to find the person who killed her brother. Like I said, she may feel more comfortable with you. Or, she may have thought of something since we spoke. She's been under a great deal of strain."

"True. I'm on it," I said, which is something he said to me quite often. "But I have a quick question for you."

He nodded.

"Why does no one talk about Belinda and Declan's mother. Is she dead?"

"I think so," he said. "I was young, and I didn't live here then. Right. I really have to go," he said.

"I could search upstairs for you."

He grinned.

"What?"

"I need to be here when that happens. If we have to make a case, there needs to be a chain of evidence. Either myself or one of my officers has to be present for a search. Right now, I don't have anyone to spare. We'll have to come back later."

"Okay."

"I'll meet you at the hospital in an hour," he said.

I nodded.

Maybe we would finally get some answers.

EIGHT

I checked with my sister at the bookstore. She was slammed, as there was more than one book club scheduled for the day.

"I can go after work, but I don't feel right leaving Caro on her own."

"That's fine," I said. "Kieran is meeting me later at the hospital. Any ideas on how I should handle Belinda?"

She sighed. "First of all, don't think of it as handling. Just be kind. You know what it is like to lose people you love. Be sympathetic and let the questions come organically so that she doesn't feel like it's the third degree."

I nodded.

"Oh, and just a minute."

I waited by the checkout counter. She came out of the office with a bouquet of flowers in a beautiful vase.

"I put these together for her this morning. I thought she might like a bit of color in that drab hospital room."

After giving Mr. Poe a good scratch behind the ears, I headed up the street to the hospital.

Belinda was there talking to her father, though he seemed to be still deep in a coma. Her eyes were red, and she appeared exhausted. Who could blame her? She'd been through the wars the last few days.

She gave me a soft smile when I came into the room.

"Morning," she said.

"Hi, my sister sent these flowers to you," I said. "She couldn't come with me because the store is busy. But she says to tell you she's thinking of you. And to please let us know if you need anything."

"Oh, that's very kind of you both. Everything feels unreal now. I can't quite wrap my mind around all that has happened."

"I can imagine. We've been through something similar, and it wasn't that long ago. Give yourself grace and time."

"You have?"

I told her about Mom, and Lizzie's fiancé and his daughter.

"Dear me, that is terrible. You are both so kind and I want you to know I'm grateful. My friends have been stopping by, of which I now consider you both. But they don't know how to talk to me. They seem uncomfortable. You and your sister are so easy to talk to. I've never been so grateful for people who are kind."

"I'm just glad we are able to help in some small way."

"It is a blessing to be surrounded by people who care, and all the members of the court have just been overwhelmingly nice. I've never eaten so much. Everyone is so lovely. My heart is broken, but it has been nice not to have to worry about my next meal or who is taking care of the farm."

"I'm guessing Joseph is helping you?"

"He is. Though he stopped by yesterday afternoon to check on me and Da."

"Oh? What time was that?"

She frowned. "I've no idea, to be honest. It was a gloomy day and the hours kind of blur together in here. He was kind enough to bring me changes of clothes, and some things from home."

If Joseph had been in town, could he have been the one who killed Declan? But why?

"He's very protective of you. He held us at gunpoint when we went to the farm."

"Oh no. I'm so sorry. I texted to let him know you were coming. That must have scared you to death."

"It was fine. Have you had any trouble with trespassers or others who should not have been on the farm?"

She shrugged. "We occasionally get the odd trespasser. But no. Since everyone knows I'm up here, though, he's probably a bit more diligent than usual."

"You may be right. I know we asked several questions the other day, but I wondered, since you have had time to sit and think for a bit, if there is anyone else you can recall who would want to cause your family harm. And I realize it's a terrible question, but I promised to help find out what is going on, so I'm very invested in finding out who killed Declan."

She pressed her lips together, as if she were trying not to cry at the mention of her brother.

"You're the one who found him, right?"

"I was. Well, our dog Mr. Poe alerted me to the situation. I'm so sorry there was nothing I could do for him."

She sniffed. "We've lived here all our lives," she said. "I don't know why anyone would want to hurt them."

I could tell, though, she was thinking about someone.

"Anything that might be relevant could be helpful," I said. "Like the man who was wanting to buy the building. Or anyone they might have had an argument with in the last few months."

"The name of the man trying to buy the building is Mac Bannon," she said. "I found his name on Da's phone. It was the only name I didn't know."

We'd already found that out, but I pretended to be shocked.

"Okay. I'll let the detective inspector know."

She had her father's phone? That would be helpful to the police.

"How do you know who he is?"

"Called the number, I did. Property development company."

"Did you speak to him?"

"I wouldn't have known what to say. So, I hung up. Though, if Da doesn't pull through, and with my brother gone..."

She sobbed and then held up a hand. "Sorry." She was choked up.

I went around the bed and gave her a hug. That was what my sister would have done.

"This is impossibly difficult, I know," I said. "I don't mean to upset you. I'm only trying to get to the heart of things."

"No. No. I understand and I'm grateful. It's just so hard."

At least Lizzie and I had each other when we were grieving. Well, we still were in a way. I couldn't imagine, even with caring friends, how alone Belinda must feel with her brother gone and her dad so ill.

"Can I ask why you had your dad's phone?"

"He left it out at the farm. I put it in my purse to bring to him next time I was in town. He had several orders and had been staying in the flat over the shop. That and I think he sometimes just likes being by himself. He and Ma used to live over the shop before they had us and moved out to the farm. The place reminds him of her."

"What happened to your mom?"

"Stroke took her when I was a baby."

"I'm so sorry. You've really been through it."

She nodded.

"Okay, so we have Mac Bannon. I'll let the detective inspector know to check him out. Anyone else? Maybe an old argument?"

She shrugged. "I mentioned him before, but I can't see him

hurting our family. But Da and Mr. Simmons have been at each other for as long as I can remember."

"The guy who owns the jewelry store in town, right?" I remembered it being closer to the shore. I'd seen Claddagh rings and other Celtic symbols in the window which had been made into necklaces and earrings. In fact, if the watch was well and truly gone, I'd thought about buying my sister a gift there for our birthday.

"Why would they be arguing?"

She smirked. "He didn't like that Da fixed jewelry. Saw us as competition. But Da has a gift for restoring things to their original state. Old Henry Simmons felt like we were stealing his business. They always had words if they ran into one another. Again, for as long as I can remember it has been like that.

"Henry's family has been designing jewelry for generations. He thought Da should have stuck to fixing clocks."

Well, that gave me some more suspects.

"Something came up while we were in the shop earlier," I said.

"Oh, what's that?"

"We found a boat dock receipt. Does your family own a boat?"

She frowned. "We do. Why?"

"Do you think it might have been where your brother was staying?"

I'd walked to the other side of the bed. She reached up and grasped her dad's hand in hers.

"It's okay," I said. "You can tell me the truth. You said you spoke to him before he died?"

She nodded.

"When?"

"In the wee hours of the morning. I lied and told you before it was by phone. I—I just wanted to protect him. I know he didn't hurt Da. Declan snuck into the hospital. He wanted to see me and Da. He'd heard the police were looking for him. But he said he had a lead on who might have hurt our father."

I could see how it would be easy to sneak into the hospital. It was small, and there was no security, as far as I had seen. If someone was away from the front desk, it would be simple to sneak past, and then out one of the side doors.

"Did he say who it was?"

"He thought it was safer for me if he didn't say."

"We mentioned last night that we found one of the glamping sites messed up. Did he stay there?"

"Friday night. He'd been in Dublin and lost his phone at the pub. He had to take a train back. He thought we were home and didn't want to wake me. He crashed at the glamping site. And then went to the boat. He said he could think more clearly there and not many people know about it. He said he didn't feel safe."

Darn him for not saying why. But there was a chance he might have left something on the boat that could give us clues.

"Would you mind if the police searched the boat? I'm sure they can get a warrant if you'd rather go that route, but it might go faster if you just give me permission."

She took her keys out of her pocket and handed me a small one off the fob. "This opens the cabin. Of course, you can search anything you want. I want to know who is determined to kill my family."

"I can ask Kieran to post someone outside the door, if that will make you feel safer."

"I heard he's understaffed. I couldn't ask him for that. I'd rather they be looking for the killer."

She might not feel right about it, but I did. Someone out there might want to finish the job with her father, and she might be on the list as well. No way I would tell her that though. She didn't need to be more paranoid. But for her safety there should have been a guard at the door.

"I'll check into that for you. If there is anyone else you can think of, please give me a call. Oh, can I take your dad's phone to the police? They might be able to find something on it."

She shrugged. "I've been through it more than once. He didn't have email. Never understood it. And he barely texted. Like I said, he only had a few names of people he called."

"Right. But you never know. I would just feel better if they could go through it as well. No stone unturned sort of thing." It was a cliché but true in this instance.

"Okay. But I want it back. He did take pictures and those I would like to keep."

"Absolutely," I said. "Is there anything else I can get you?"

"No. But do tell your sister thank you for the flowers. They are beautiful. I'm grateful that you've been looking into things and that you found—" She sniffed hard. "That you found my brother. I pray he wasn't lying there for long. I hate thinking of him that way. Did the police say how he died? Or do you know?"

"I don't for sure. It looked like he'd been hit on the head. Not unlike your father. But there will be an autopsy, and hopefully that will tell us more. I keep saying this, but I'm very sorry you're going through this."

There was a knock on the door. It was my neighbor, Lolly. Today, she was dressed from head to toe in a pine green. She was always so colorful, and I loved that about her.

"Oh, I didn't know you'd be here, Mercy." Her enormous Irish Wolfhound, Bernard, was with her. I was surprised they'd let him in. But she had narcolepsy, and he was a true service dog, who protected her while she slept. He went everywhere with her.

"I'm just heading out," I said.

"I brought plenty of scones to share," she said. She glanced from me to Belinda.

"Thank you, but I need to be going. I promised to meet your grandson soon."

Lolly gave me a smile and her eyes twinkled.

What is that about?

I headed out of the hospital. Kieran was just outside in his SUV. When he saw me, he jumped out of the car and ran around to open the passenger door.

"Thanks," I said.

When he returned to the driver's side, I told him everything.

"Interesting," he said.

"Do you have an evidence bag?"

He reached into the back seat and handed me one.

"What did you find?"

I slipped the phone into the clear bag. "This is her father's. He'd left it out at the farm. She says there isn't much on it, but I thought you might want your tech guys to take a look at it. She also gave me a few names to check out. Plus, I have the boat keys. Her brother was staying there for a few hours. Why don't we check that first, and I'll tell you about the rest of the suspects on the way?"

He smiled. "You have been busy."

"You have no idea."

NINE

As Kieran drove down to the boat docks, I told him about the property developer, the jewelry maker. That along with the fact they had feud with the farm next door, gave us too many suspects.

Today the detective inspector wore one of his cable-knit sweaters over jeans and was handsome as always. We'd had a rough start when my sister and I moved to Shamrock Cove, but we'd become closer as we solved cases together. There was no one I trusted more. And while I'd never admit it to him, I enjoyed spending time with him. He was smart, and had my dark sense of humor.

"The Donnels and the Flynns have been fighting for years," he said. "Though I've never taken it seriously. Most of their scuffles happen after too much drink at the pub. The glamping sites are just the latest complaints."

"Right, but that doesn't mean they aren't suspects," I said. "Someone was angry enough to attack both of the Flynn men. Those sorts of festering relations can often end in violence."

He chuckled.

"What's so funny?"

"Nothing. It's just you sound like you're writing one of your books."

Well, I had to admit this case had my creative brain burning to write it all down. I never wrote true crime or used it for inspiration for books. But working these cases did help my imagination.

"I'm never not a writer," I said. "It's the way I'm made."

"Didn't say there was anything wrong with it, did I? All that research you do makes you a fount of knowledge that I've come to appreciate."

I grinned, and he glanced at me.

"What are you smiling at?"

"The fact that you hated this fount of knowledge when we first met. You thought I was meddling."

"You were meddling into a dangerous situation."

"And saved you from the killer."

"You did. Which is why I've grown to quite enjoy our chats and investigations."

My stomach fluttered. I stared out the window, but I couldn't stop smiling. "Me too. I think it is kind of awful that I'm inspired by someone else's tragedy. But maybe that is why I'm so determined to help."

"Could be. Also, while you may be curiously inspired, you're also a kind person who believes in justice."

I laughed.

He pulled up along the dock that led to the marina. Before I could get out, he was at my door. I didn't mind chivalry and never complained. His grandmother Lolly would have words if she ever heard he wasn't being a gentleman to a woman. It didn't matter if it was me or someone else.

I followed him down the steep steps leading to where the boats were in various-sized slips.

There was a small, wooden building next to the stairs. A

man slid a window open. "Hello, Detective Inspector. How can I help you today?"

"I'm looking for the Flynns' boat," he said. "I have permission to take a look."

"Lovely people," he said. "Terrible tragedy. Boat is the *Lady Marie*, slip seven." He pointed in what I assumed was the general direction.

"Thank you, Stephen. You haven't by any chance seen anything abnormal. Anyone on the boat that shouldn't be, that sort of thing?"

"Not that I know of. Though we don't have anyone covering nights, and I leave at five. Been short-handed since Clancy moved to Dingle."

Kieran sighed.

"But we do have cameras. If you give me a date and time, I can make a copy for you."

"Excellent," Kieran said. He gave the man some parameters.

"I'll get on this for you."

At the boat slip, I was surprised. It was a fair-sized cruiser.

"I was expecting a small sailboat," I said. "That's what I get for assuming."

"I think as part of the glamping experience, they offered fishing expeditions and island tours," Kieran said. He helped me onto the boat. I was grateful I was in my rubber-soled boots today.

"Do you have the key?" he asked.

I handed it to him.

He opened the indoor cabin. There was a small sofa and couple of sleeping berths. A tiny toilet was in the rear of the cabin.

He handed me a pair of gloves. "You start in here. I'm heading up to the captain's nest to see if I can find anything. They also should have kept a log of the last time they went out. Keep an eye out. Let me know what you find."

He handed over some evidence bags. "These are for anything important. I'll log whatever you find later."

"Okay. That's a lot of trust you are putting in me." I smiled.

"There aren't many I would trust more." He turned and left.

I stared after him. Yes, we'd come a long way since I first arrived in Shamrock Cove, and he had suspected me of murder.

Across from the table and booth where people could eat, were several drawers. I opened each one carefully. The first one was full of papers. I pulled them out and then sat down at the booth to look at them.

Then I rolled my eyes. If Kieran did call in forensics, I'd probably just messed up a load of prints. I was new to this investigating-for-real business, and I had a lot to learn. It was much easier solving fictional crimes.

The boat license was in the elder Mr. Flynn's name. But there were other licenses for the younger one, and his sister, to captain the boat. There were several receipts for gas and food. It looked like they provided snacks for their guests during the excursions.

There were manuals for the boat and engine. And warranties for the various gadgets. Nothing that really stood out. There were some hooks on the wall where something had hung, but it was long gone.

I put everything back and went on to the next drawer. Again, nothing. The bottom drawer was a bit more interesting.

"Oh. Wow. I did not see this coming."

TEN

I called out for Kieran to come down and then I carefully picked up one of the items I had found. It was exactly what I thought. But why would he have these things here? Was there more than one answer? I didn't think so.

"What did you—? Is that what I think it is?" he asked.

I nodded. "It's the watch I took in to get fixed. And it's working. Mr. Flynn must have fixed it. Did Declan rob his own store?"

"It appears that way," he said. "But let's not jump to conclusions. These items might have also been planted by the killer. Or he could have had an altercation with them and taken the items."

I cocked my head and stared up at him. "I'm usually the one who says that sort of thing."

He shrugged. "I've known Declan most of my life. While he liked his drink, he was as good as they come. And he loved his family. I can't see him hurting his da. None of this makes sense."

"Maybe he was doing it for insurance purposes. Your team is going through his financials. Have they found anything?"

He nodded. "Looks like they were struggling, but most do

during the down season. Things pick up when the tourists start coming back. They were barely making it, but they were surviving. And the farm does quite well all year round. They sell wool, as well as the caravan and camping sites on the property. Those are only down one month a year, right before summer, to do any sort of rehab or repairs. That's why they have no one staying there now. So far, it looks like that side of the family business was doing well."

I pursed my lips.

"What is it?"

"I haven't known them as long as you have, but I agree. There is no way Declan would have hurt his father. But what if he knew someone might rob the store, and took these items out to hide them, just leaving the clocks behind? They are larger and harder to hide."

"That's quite the stretch," he said.

"You keep saying that but stay with me. Is it possible he owed someone money? Maybe he planned to let them rob the store. They would get the items, and he would get the insurance."

"But then why kill Declan?"

"Perhaps the thief found out what he did. When Declan didn't pony up the goods, he was murdered."

"Pony up the goods? You sound like an American gangster."

"I'm not a gangster, but I'm still American." I smiled. "It's all so confusing though. And we can't ask him because he's gone. I'm guessing all these items will have to go into evidence."

"You are correct. Since they were technically stolen. But I'll see if I can clear the watch for you. I just don't know if it will be in time for your birthday next week."

I frowned.

"What is it?"

"How do you know when my birthday is?"

He glanced away and then cleared his throat. "You mentioned it when you told me about the watch."

"Um. No. I told you it was coming up, but I didn't mention the date."

"I'm certain you did," he said. He pretended to look into the small pantry by the galley sink.

"No. You know about the surprise party, don't you?"

"Again, no idea why you would think that." He refused to look at me.

"It's been rattling around in my brain. My friends know how much I dislike that sort of thing. But Lizzie—"

"That's probably why she told us all not to tell you. And if we did, she told us to say it was Brenna, Rob, and Lolly planning things. She will be very upset with me if she finds out I was the one who told you. Maybe you could pretend to be surprised."

I sighed. "I don't want to disappoint her, but I've never been a big fan of surprises like that. Or being the center of attention."

"But you're a famous author. You're always the center of attention."

I laughed. "Only at events and signings, and it isn't my favorite part of the job. Don't get me wrong. I love talking with fans and to anyone who loves books as much as I do. But speaking engagements and signings wear me out quickly. I'd rather be in my office writing. Or in our library reading."

"Or watching your UK mysteries."

I laughed. "True. Speaking of writing... I should get back to it sometime today." There was a deadline with my name on it at the end of the month, and I was only a quarter of the way finished with the novel.

"Promise you won't tell your sister you found out about the party from me. She and Gran have been working on surprising you. I'll never hear the end of it."

"Well, since you've been so kind to let me help with the

case, I guess I can pretend. Also, Brenna, Lolly and Rob already mentioned it. They understand how I feel. So, you weren't the first."

"Thanks," he said. He handed me his logbook. "Do you mind logging in the evidence you found? I'm going to check the engine room downstairs."

"Is that legal? I mean, aren't you worried about the chain of evidence?"

"The paperwork for you to be a part-time consultant went through, so technically, you're in the clear."

"Wait. What? You were serious about that? I thought you might be messing around."

"Well, after you nearly got yourself killed, more than once, I thought it might be safer to work with you in a more official capacity."

"Were you going to tell me or were you just covering your butt?"

He shrugged. "Now you know."

"Thanks." I was secretly pleased that he trusted me so much. I loved working with him, and now I would have an excuse to do it even more. I couldn't stop grinning.

He headed down through a hatch in the floor, and we spent another hour on the boat. I kept staring at the walls in the small cabin where there was a galley kitchen, and a table. At the bow of the boat was a sleeping berth big enough for two.

But something felt off. I glanced around at the walls. There wasn't much décor. There were a few empty hooks that appeared to be utilitarian. Since I'd never been here before, I had no idea what might have hung there. I made some notes in my journal.

I had logged everything by the time Kieran finished with his search. Except for the jewelry, we hadn't found anything else.

We headed back to his car. "I need to get the evidence back

to the station, and this logbook of the trips they took on the boat. I want to make certain they coincide with the tours."

"Do you think maybe they were smuggling or something?"

He laughed. "You've definitely been watching too much television again. No. I don't. As I said, I've known them my whole life. But I have to cover the bases, as you like to say. I believe that's a baseball term. Not as fun as cricket, but it is interesting."

I laughed.

"While you're doing that, you could drop me off at the jewelry store owned by Henry Simmons," I said.

"I thought we agreed we'd do these things together."

"And we will," I said. "But I need to buy a different gift for my sister in case you need to keep the watch for some reason. If he's there, he might open up to someone he thinks is just a customer."

He nodded. "You may have a point there. Be careful, though. Henry isn't the kindest man. He's known for being a curmudgeon. The long-time feud with the Flynns may be a sore subject."

"Understood," I said.

"So, you'll be careful?"

"Yes." I sighed. I wouldn't complain that he was worried about my safety. I hadn't always been careful in the past.

He stopped at the end of Main Street and ran to open the door for me.

All I had to do was cross the street, as the Simmons's store was the first one past the Shamrock Cove beach. The wind had picked up and I pulled the hood of my mac over my head.

"Tread lightly," he said.

"I appreciate your concern, but this isn't the first time I've interviewed a witness. Besides, I'll be spending money in his store. Also, I met him a few times at the pub quiz. He calls me the famous author and swears he loves my books."

"Fine. Like I said, though, just watch yourself."

"You keep saying that in different ways. He's not going to shoot me dead in the middle of his store."

"Don't say things like that," he said.

"You sound like my sister."

"Well, she is the sensible one," he said under his breath.

Then we both laughed.

"I'll text you when I'm finished shopping."

He waited until I crossed the street before pulling away. He was protective like that.

Instead of a bell over the door like most of the shops, there was a chime on Simmons's Jewelers. It sounded like an overly long doorbell.

There was no one inside. Not even a clerk. So, I stood there waiting.

"Hello?" I called out.

No one was there. Something didn't feel right. I started to call Kieran to come back, but I didn't want to worry him for no reason.

There was a room behind the counters. I lifted the piece of wood on the side and stepped through.

When I made it to the back room, I gasped.

"Not again."

ELEVEN

There in the back room of the jewelry store, a man was slumped over on the desk. I raced over to check his pulse. But when I did, he jumped up and screamed. He wasn't the only one. I thought he'd been dead.

"What are you doing?" he roared.

"I thought maybe you were ill or..." Dead. But I didn't finish my sentence. "No one answered when I came in and I was worried."

"Can't a man get some rest during his lunch hour? Can you not read the sign? And how did you get in?"

I followed him to the front of the store.

"There was no sign and the door was unlocked."

He stared at the door. "Jessie. Doesn't have a brain God gave a bat."

Bats were highly intelligent and instinctive, but it didn't seem the right time to tell him that.

"You're the novelist," he said. "I'm a grump when I first wake up. This isn't your fault. Jessie evidently went out for a late lunch and forgot the sign and to lock the door. I'm lucky we weren't robbed blind. I keep telling the girl she has to learn responsibility. She's my daughter. Great when it comes to creating original pieces, but she has her ma's artist brain, always a bit scattered. We have a booth at the fête, and she's very behind on the planning.

"But enough of that. How can I help you?"

I told him about taking my watch to get fixed for my sister, and that it was stolen. I didn't mention it was found.

"Told old Flynn years ago that he needed to up his security. Tried to compete with me, as if. I'm sorry for your loss, but I'm sure we can find something suitable."

I didn't want to buy anything from this grumpy man, but I was also desperate for a new gift.

"I read about the Claddagh rings. I know they are usually for couples, but I know my sister has been wanting one. It's one of her favorite designs."

"Ah." He waved his hand over one of the glass counters. "We have gold, silver and ones with gemstones. They can repre-sent familial love as well. We have myths and legends to cover most of our Celtic heritage in various ways."

"Did you know the Flynns well?" It wasn't much of a segue. "I mean, I heard the elder Mr. Flynn is in the hospital and isn't doing well. Then there is his poor son. I'm the one who found him. Rather, my dog did."

"Oh?" He appeared interested. "Terrible. Terrible. I do hope Flynn wakes from his coma, but he'll be heartbroken over his son. We may not be the best of friends, but I wouldn't wish that on anyone. Losing a child is the worst thing that could happen to a parent."

He appeared sincere. And his brows drew together in sadness. He meant what he'd said.

"Would you be wanting gold or silver?" he asked.

"Let's look at the silver ones. She likes the color better."

"I have some with gemstones as well, and a few with diamonds."

He wasn't wrong. In addition to the rings, the room was surrounded by several glass cases with all kinds of jewelry from wedding sets to fancy watches. There were also some pretty necklaces with Celtic symbols. While he was turned away, I took a photo. I wanted to look the symbols up online.

"These are beautiful," I said. "What is that purple stone?" I thought it might be Alexandrite, which was our birthstone. It was very hard to find and was usually artificially made. He confirmed my suspicions.

"But this is the real deal. Expensive, but will only grow in value. It's a great investment."

"I'll take it," I said. My sister would be furious if she found out how much it cost. But she was worth it. If the watch did become available in time for the party, then I'd save the ring for Christmas. At least, I'd be covered one way or another.

He wrapped it up in a beautiful package. Now, I just had to sneak by the bookstore and pray Lizzie didn't see me.

"Oh, one more thing," I said.

"What's that?" He seemed much more amenable since I'd spent some money in his shop.

"I know you weren't close, but is there anyone you know of who might want to cause the Flynns trouble? I'm just curious since I found them both. It seems like everyone I've spoken to adored them. I just don't understand how anyone could hurt them."

He shrugged. "Can't help you there. Though I would like to know myself. If we have thieves in town, they need to be caught. Especially before our biggest season. That sort of thing is bad PR for the town."

I would bet my house he had no idea how selfish he sounded.

"I do remember Declan getting caught up with a bad crowd when he was younger. He was going to university in Dublin. His dad insisted he come home and help out with the family business. Claimed heart trouble at the time. Looks like, he might have been serious since he had a heart attack. At least, that's what I've heard."

"Oh. Did Declan clean up his act?"

"Seemed to," he said. "I don't know their business, but one hears things in town and at the pub. The last few years, he seemed to keep his nose clean."

I wondered if he was right. Had Declan's past come back to haunt him?

I'd have to ask Kieran what he knew.

He handed me the small gift bag. "Come back to see us," he said.

I stuck the bag in the large inside pocket of my mac. Seemed the safest place since I had to pass by the bookstore on my way home.

"Thank you."

I left the store, and it was pouring down rain. I pulled my hood up. I made it to the corner where the scent of coffee and baked goods caught my attention. My stomach grumbled and I laughed.

Time to feed the beast.

Paisley's Bakery was on the corner. Paisley had just reopened her patisserie shop after refurbishing the interior. It was like one of those tiny shops one found in Paris. Everything in a deep green from the walls to the tables. There were small, black bistro tables inside. And this time of day she always had a lovely selection of sandwiches and soups, along with her high-end patisserie in the tall glass cases.

I ordered a chicken salad sandwich to go, and half a dozen treats. I promised myself I'd save at least a few of the treats for my sister. She was also a big fan of the place. When the line died down, Paisley brought my food over in a white bag tied with a blue ribbon.

"I have something to tell you," she whispered.

"Oh?"

"I heard you found both the Flynns, and I think I know what might have happened."

The bell over her door rang as a customer came inside. "Let me serve them and I'll be right back," she said.

I wasn't going anywhere. Why would she know anything about the Flynns? I was curious to find out.

The customer left, and she locked the door behind them and put the closed sign up, even though she had several hours to go.

"I could come back later," I said. Though I was anxious to know what she'd meant.

"I usually take an hour break in the afternoon. I'm under-staffed at the moment. I've hired some university students, but I have a few days until they are done with their exams. And we've all the planning for the fête. It's been a bit wild."

I nodded.

"Right, so, Jessie is a friend of mine. We went to school together years ago," she said.

"Jessie, Mr. Simmons the jeweler's daughter?"

"That's the one," she said.

"What about her?"

"Well, and I feel terrible for saying this because he's dead—God rest his soul."

"Declan?"

"Yes."

"What about him?" I leaned into hear her. Even though we were alone, she'd lowered her voice.

"They were dating. She and Declan."

Well, that was a shocker.

"How do you know?"

"She told me. They liked to sneak away to his boat to get away from the world and so their fathers wouldn't find out.

She'd grab some of my sandwiches and treats when they had their... well, you know. Uh. Dates."

"Right."

"I'm betting old man Simmons found out. Went after Declan but caused the older one to have a heart attack. Probably bashed his head in when he fell. Then he killed Declan."

"Why do you think he could do all of that?"

"Have you met him? He's not a nice man. Jessie is a sweetheart. Takes after her ma, who was also a sweetheart. But her da. I wouldn't put it past him. She was afraid what he might do if he found out about them.

"And I happen to know she was in Dublin with Declan the night the store was broken into. She thought he might propose. They had talked about running away and getting married. That way they wouldn't have to deal with their families."

This was a lot of new information. My brain tried to process it.

"Have you told any of this to Kieran?"

"No. I can't know for sure, can I? It's all hearsay and I wouldn't want to bug him. I haven't seen her since she left for Dublin with him. I was surprised he came back to town. I thought this was when they were making a run for it. Well, I mean, he came back because of his dad, right?"

"But if you have info, you should share it with the police," I said.

"Well, I'm talking to you, aren't I? You'll let him know what I said. That Kieran likes proof of things. Doesn't like... what's the word? Supposition, I think it is. But they were good at hiding their relationship. What if one of the fathers found out and tried to kill the other?"

She had a point and was right about Kieran. He would want the facts.

"Is there anyone else you know of who might want to hurt the Flynns?"

She made a face.

"What is it?"

"Well, running a shop where the public is involved, I hear all sorts of gossip."

"But you're thinking of something that involves the Flynns directly?"

She nodded.

"Tell me. Any information might be helpful, and I promise the police will thoroughly vet it before taking action."

Or I would. And then I would tell Kieran. Like I had said, she was right. He would want the facts.

"The Donnels have the farm next one over from the Flynns."

"Right."

"Well, Declan was keen to sell to them. He wasn't a big fan of the part of the family business selling wool or the caravan park. His sister and Da were against it. I know from Belinda, they were doing well. We've been friends since I came back from Paris. I adore her. And I hate all of this. I'm just trying to help. Please, don't think I'm like the rest of the gossips around here."

"You don't think his family killed him, do you?" I couldn't have imagined his sister doing anything like that.

"No. Not the Flynns. But the Donnels might be upset if they said no. Perhaps they thought if they got the males out of the way poor Belinda might be more willing to sell."

"So, you think one of the Donnels may have done this?"

"Listen to me. I sound like I'm trying to write one of your crime novels. I'm just sharing what I've heard. And if the Flynns did sell, who would be out of a job?"

"Joseph," I whispered.

She nodded. "It could have been any of them. Again, please don't think I'm a gossip. And I don't usually share anything that is said in my shop. But I adore the Flynns and Jessie. I don't want anyone else to get hurt. At the very least I thought maybe, since I know you're working with the detective inspector, you could hint about the troubles."

I'd be doing a lot more than hinting.

"I will do my best."

She clasped my hands in hers. "I knew I could count on you. If you hadn't come to the shop by today, I'd promised myself to visit number three, so I could tell you what I knew."

"I'm grateful."

"I'm glad to have got all that off my chest, and I hope I'm wrong. I don't like the idea of our villagers hurting one another. But the Donnels are a bit rough. They... might do whatever it takes to get what they want. They've done it before with other farmers. Belinda is so sweet. She might be easily pressured with the rest of her family gone. And Joseph is very protective of her. If he thought someone might try to hurt her... well, you know."

I didn't really but I nodded. She'd added some suspects to the list. Well, a better case for some of the suspects than we already had. Now, we had to eliminate them one by one with alibis and information.

She glanced outside. Even though it was raining, there was a line of people around the corner. Her patisserie was outstanding.

"I should get back to it," she said. She unlocked the door and flipped the sign. "Welcome," she said as she held the door open.

Before I left, I texted Kieran. He didn't answer, which probably meant he was on a call. Sharing my new information would have to wait. I told him to come by number three when he had some time.

I headed home with my goodies. But I felt guilty when passing the bookstore. I went in to see if my sister needed anything. She was at the register checking out several people in line, as Caro wrapped gifts.

I waited for them to finish. Even though my stomach growled so loud the customers turned to look at me.

"I thought you were writing today?"

"I am. I had to go get reinforcements." I held up the bag, and she and Caro laughed. "But I'm happy to share. I wanted to make sure you didn't need anything."

"Business has been busy this morning. Mr. Poe has been a bit anxious. He could maybe use a run in the backyard, if you don't mind."

He barked.

"Of course I don't mind. I'm betting he would also like to curl up in front of the fire at my office."

He barked again.

"Come get what you want from the patisserie and then I'll take him home." He glanced up at the box as I pulled it from the bag.

"Not for you," Lizzie said. "The vet said we had to stop with the treats. But if you are a good boy, and let Mercy write, you can have a treat after."

I swear he understood every word she said and actually smirked at me. He knew I'd give him a treat as soon as we arrived at the house. My sister could resist his sweet puppy eyes. I was a born sucker where Mr. Poe was concerned.

After putting on his lead, we headed out the back door. It was still raining, though it was more of a mist now.

I was about to push in the secret door that led to the bailey of the castle where we lived when Poe barked, and I jumped.

I turned to see where his menacing growl was directed. But no one was there.

My sister and I had felt like someone might be following us since we'd moved to Ireland. It wasn't all the time, but enough that it made us wary. I'd thought it might have been the stalker I had in New York. But that was before we found out our dad might be alive.

"Is that you, Dad? Please, if it is, come out of hiding. Lizzie and I would like to meet you."

I was met with an eerie silence. I felt silly, until Mr. Poe's growl became more menacing. I decided I'd had enough and pushed inside the stone wall. When I was on the other side, I leaned against it with all my weight to stop anyone from following.

But no one tried to open the secret door.

"Am I imagining things?" I asked Mr. Poe.

He barked, as if to say no.

Someone had been there, but who?

TWELVE

Later that evening, there was a knock on the door. Lizzie had gone for a quick drink with Brenna, so I knew it wasn't her. Though she sometimes forgot her key. Mr. Poe wiggled but didn't bark, which meant he was excited to visit a friend.

I opened the small door that served as a peephole and found Kieran staring back at me. "You said to come by," he said. "I brought food from the pub. I saw Lizzie with Brenna when I stopped by to see if you were there. She suggested you probably haven't eaten."

I hadn't since my late lunch. But I could always eat.

"That was kind of you," I said as I opened the door wider for him to come through. Mr. Poe tried to trip him up in his excitement.

"Okay, boy. I see you," Kieran said as he handed me the bag of food. Then he knelt to give our dog a good scratch around the ears. Mr. Poe was in heaven. He adored the detective inspector.

"Come on back to the kitchen. I have so much information for you. I don't know where to start." I'd been good about waiting to speak to Kieran before I made an effort to talk to the rest of the suspects. He'd been including me in all of this, and I didn't want to mess that up.

I'd spent all afternoon writing my next book, which was due soon. But I had to stop a few times and write down my thoughts about our current case in my notebook.

"Go ahead to the kitchen. I need to get my notebook from my office. I don't want to forget anything."

By the time I made it to the rear of the house, he'd already pulled out silverware and plates for us.

I grinned. He'd made himself at home, which I didn't mind at all. We had been spending a great deal of time together and I enjoyed his company.

"Oh, is it shepherd's pie night?"

"It is." He smiled.

Matt and his mom, who owned the pub, made amazing food and coffee, along with their drinks. The Crown and Clover was a popular place with locals and visitors for a reason.

"Decaf?" I asked. It was after seven.

"Seems like a sacrilege with that machine, but yes."

He was as big a fan of my coffee machine—a Jura Giga Ten —as I was. It was a splurge but worth every penny.

We ate in silence for a few minutes, and then I put my fork down. I opened my notebook. I told him about my visit with Mr. Simmons.

"That is interesting." He sounded more curious than anything.

"The chance to chat just presented itself."

He grunted, but didn't say anything. I continued with my story. "He said he wouldn't wish the death of a child on anyone," I said. "He seemed to really be upset about that. He isn't the nicest person. I've heard that from more than one source. But I'm not sure I can see him trying to kill the Flynns."

"Someone succeeded with Declan Flynn."

"I know. But that is what I'm saying. He seemed very upset

by that. There was no love lost, but he couldn't imagine losing a child like that. His distress was real."

"I'll look into it."

"Well, you should. There is even more to the story," I said.

I told him everything Paisley had told me.

"How did you know to even ask her?"

I laughed. "I didn't have to. I swear, she offered it up. Even closed her shop for fifteen minutes so no one else would hear us."

"What is it?"

"You've learned more in an hour today than we have in the last two days. At least, we have some more info on our leads."

I shrugged. "I'm just glad it's helpful—or at least, I hope it will be. What do you know about the Donnels?"

He sighed. "She's not exaggerating there. They like to do things their way with little concern for the law. Though the most we've ever caught them on is DUIs and a few fights in the pub. Drunk and disorderly should be their middle names. Only one of them was ever charged with assault. The witnesses tend to stay silent when it comes to them."

"So, they are bullies?"

"Yes. Though they don't come into town that often. I could see them putting the pressure on the Flynns about the property. They were never fans of the caravan and glamping sites. Thought they were a blight. They believe the land should be preserved for the animals and farming."

"Well, you can't really fault them there," I said. "Lots of people are trying to preserve the heritage of their land."

"Right. But people also need to make a living. Bullying is never a good thing."

"I one hundred percent agree with you there, which is why I didn't go out to their place alone."

"I'd rather you didn't. I'll be handling that with someone on my team. I don't want you mixed up with that crowd."

I frowned. "I thought we were working on this together." I sounded like a petulant child. But my curiosity had been piqued. I wanted to meet with all the players in our drama. It was the only way my mind could sort them into categories. Guilty. Not guilty. Or possibly guilty.

He held up a hand. "I think it might be better if you question Belinda again. Find out if she knew anything about her brother and Jessie. As much as you might think it wasn't Henry Simmons, fathers will do most anything to protect their children. I've seen a great deal in my line of work. It's possible, since she was close to her brother, that Declan might have shared something.

"But you have confirmed for us that he wasn't alone in Dublin. The timeline we've put together is that he most likely heard about his dad in the wee hours of Friday morning and headed back here. DNA puts him in the yurt and then the boat. We still haven't processed everything from the sites though. Maybe there will be more leading to our killer."

"Did you find anything under his fingernails? Or did whoever is doing the autopsy? I always worry that if someone's DNA isn't in a database somewhere, there would be no way of knowing who the real killer is. I use that a lot in my books. It keeps the suspense going."

He smiled. "They are still doing the testing. We have a few preliminary findings, but nothing solid yet, as you like to say."

Did I say solid? I didn't think I used it much, but I did in my books. I remembered my editor, Carrie, picking it out once.

"Kieran?"

He glanced up from his plate.

"What?"

"Have you been reading my books?"

His eyes went wide, and his cheeks were pink.

He shrugged. "Sheila suggested, since we were working together, that I read some of your books."

"Sheila said that?"

He nodded.

"And? I'm not fishing for compliments, but as a law enforcement officer I'm curious what you think about them."

"Honestly, you get a great deal of the procedural elements correct, more so than most. I appreciate that." I had a feeling that was as close to a compliment as I was going to get.

"Thanks. What about Jessie?"

"What about her?"

"Don't you think we should talk to her?"

"Yes, but we would need to do it away from her father, don't you think? And like Belinda, she might respond better if it's just you and, maybe, Lizzie."

"Why Lizzie?"

"I've seen Jessie in your store, more than once."

I held up a finger. "She might belong to one of the book clubs as well. Though, if she's grieving, she might not show up."

"People are habitual creatures," he said. "More often than not, they go back to their lives because it gives them a sense of sameness from before the tragedy. I see it all the time in my work. People don't want to sit at home with their thoughts."

He was right. Jessie had gone back to work that morning. Her father had said she'd left the door open and forgot to put up the sign. Though she had to be grieving if she had heard the news about Declan.

"I'll check with my sister about that. Worst case, Lizzie can put together one of her baskets that she does for people. We could say we heard it from a trusted source, but we won't share it with anyone else."

"Except me."

I nodded. "Of course."

We finished our food and then I asked him the question that was at the forefront of my mind.

"Are Lizzie and I safe? I mean, Declan got in here even with our new security system. And someone killed him right outside our gate."

"Which is why Lolly had cameras installed along the back lane. They are hidden in the trees but will be monitored by the station. The walkway is public. So, we can do that."

"Remind me not to run around nude in the backyard."

He coughed and nearly spat out his coffee.

I handed him another napkin. Then we laughed.

"Is that something you do often?"

I shrugged. "Only under the light of the full moon or an eclipse."

He laughed hard. "Good to know. But the cameras are facing the back lane, and there is a sign posted on the hill that the space is now covered by CCTV. Lolly hopes it will keep the hooligans—her word—from hanging out back there."

"I'm all about more security," I said.

"You should be since you're constantly finding yourself in trouble."

I smirked. "It's not like I look for it."

"Oh, I'm more than aware. It has a habit of finding you."

"I forgot something," I said. "And I promised to tell you everything."

His brows drew together with worry. "What is it?"

"When we were coming home tonight, I swear someone was watching me again. Mr. Poe even growled. He sensed it too."

He flipped his notebook open again and wrote something down. "Did you see anyone?"

"I looked, but the foggy mist made it difficult to see very far."

"Do you think it might be your father?"

I sat up straighter. "Why? Have there been sightings?"

"Not that I know of," he said. "But we'll also be putting nine cameras on the back alley. We should have done that years ago. Crime has never been a problem here."

I sighed. "I know. Until Lizzie and I arrived."

He smiled. "I didn't mean it like that."

"Will people blame us?" I'd always been curious about that. We did seem to find way more dead bodies than any people should in their lifetime.

"No. But they do believe Mr. Poe is a great detective."

I laughed.

"That he is."

"Just do me a favor," he said.

"What's that?"

"Don't interview the suspects without either me or your sister with you. I'd feel better if you didn't go into these situations alone. Well, except for Jessie."

I understood why. I'd found myself in more trouble when I struck out on my own.

And if whoever had been watching me wasn't my dad, then... I shivered. Kieran was right. I may have accidentally asked someone the wrong question. And I didn't want to be next on the hit list.

THIRTEEN

After making certain Caro could cover the store the next morning, Lizzie and I went back to the hospital. I had updated her on everything Kieran and I had discovered so far. While she was usually more wary than I was when it came to investigating, she was just as intrigued and curious to find out who could have hurt the lovely Flynns. Those were her words.

She'd put together another basket of baked goods, as well as a care package with various things that Belinda might need. Like a soft blanket, some magazines, and other things that could bring her comfort. I wasn't an unfeeling jerk, but my sister had that nurturing side where giving came naturally. Whereas I had to do pros and cons lists and worry what someone might think if I gave them the wrong thing.

When we arrived, we found Belinda alone in the room.

Did he die? My heart was in my throat.

Lizzie rushed in and hugged Belinda, who was sobbing. "What happened?"

"They've rushed him off for tests. Something happened again with his heart. It doesn't look good. He's already so weak. The surgeon says it would be pointless to try and fix him up until he's stronger. Or something like that. What am I going to do if I lose him, too? This isn't fair. I'm trying to stay positive but I'm so scared."

"Anyone would be," Lizzie said. "We are here for you."

Belinda sobbed into my sister's shoulder. I put the basket down on a side table and then stood there not really knowing what to do. Joining the hug didn't feel right. Again, something my sister was better at than I was.

"What's happened?" a male voice said behind me. I turned to see it was Joseph. His voice was loud and rough. The two women hugging jumped.

"It's Da," Belinda sniffled. "It doesn't look good. They've taken him for some tests."

Joseph frowned. He held a bouquet of wildflowers in a ball jar vase. "I brought these for you... and, uh, your da," he said. He shoved them toward her. She took them.

"Thank you, Joseph."

"Welcome. Do you need anything from the house?"

She sniffled. "No. I'm good. Thank you."

He stood there as awkwardly as I did. Poor guy. I felt sorry for him. It was obvious he cared about her. It was written all over his face. Some of us didn't know what to do when those close to us were grieving so hard. Not that I didn't grieve. I did my fair share the last year, but I was usually in my room alone.

She gave him a watery smile.

This was most definitely not the best time to question her about her brother. Even I understood that.

"We brought some baked goods," my sister said. "Would you like tea or coffee to go with them?" she asked Belinda.

"Oh, I'd love a cuppa. Mine's gone cold." Her face was red, but the tears had stopped. My sister really was wonderful at looking after people.

"Mercy and Joseph, would you mind?" Did I mention my

sister was brilliant at getting people to do things? She was so kind about it, no one ever questioned her intentions.

But this was her way of getting Belinda alone. And me alone with Joseph. I needed to ask him about the Donnels.

We headed to the small café at the front of the hospital.

"It's kind of you to check on her," I said.

He shrugged. "She loves her da and brother. She's going to have a very hard time if she loses them both." He sounded quite worried about her.

"Let's hope that doesn't happen. Maybe they'll find out what's going on with Mr. Flynn."

"We can hope," he said. He was gruff but seemed to have a good heart. He cared about her and the family. That much was evident.

"You still working with the police?" he asked.

"I am. Why? Do you have information?"

"No. Went to school with Declan. His family was better to me than my own. Been working on that farm since I was a young lad. I could have never imagined something like this would happen. Everyone loves them."

"It's really awful." I wasn't sure where he was going with all of this.

"It is."

"You said everyone loves them, but do you know anyone who would want to cause them harm? I know you've been asked, but sometimes things come to us after we've had time to think a bit on them. I heard a rumor about the Donnels. Or Mr. Simmons, who owns the jewelry store. I just want to make sure Belinda is safe."

I sounded like a terrible gossip, which I was not. But in this village, it was one of the main ways people communicated. I had to put my personal feelings aside. Also, I'd learned it was helpful when investigating crimes. More often than not, there was a grain of truth in rumors that sometimes produced results.

He glanced at me and frowned. "What about the Simmonses?"

Hmm. Interesting that was the name he picked up on. I would have thought he'd be more curious about the Donnels.

"That Jessie and Declan were seeing each other."

His eyes went wide. "What?" He wasn't angry, more surprised. "Jessie Simmons?"

I nodded. "Yes. Obviously, you didn't know."

"I can't imagine any of us knew. If Mr. Flynn hadn't had a heart attack, that would give him one. There is bad blood between those families."

"I've heard that. But I do believe it's true. They've been seen together more than once, and were both in Dublin the night of the break-in."

"No. I can't say any of them knew. I feel like if he said something to Belinda, she would have told me."

There was a queue at the café. So, we had to wait our turn.

He blew out a breath.

"Do you think old man Simmons found out and killed him? I wouldn't put it past him."

I shrugged. "I don't think so. Declan seemed like he could hold his own in a fight." Though someone had bettered him behind our home.

"He was hit from behind, right?"

"Who told you that?"

"Heard it in the pub last night," he said. "One of the police officers were in there and Matt asked him what happened."

I'd have to tell poor Kieran about that. The last thing he needed was information about the case getting out to possible suspects. I'd text him later. I felt sorry if he figured out who the officer in the pub had been.

"Coward, hitting someone from behind. Also heard you found him."

"My dog, Mr. Poe, did. I tried to help him, but it was too late."

"Sad business all around. Belinda is strong, but this…"

"I lost my mom last year and we also lost my sister's fiancé and his daughter. Family is everything."

"It is. She's going to be all alone," he whispered.

"Is she?" I asked, and I cocked my head.

He frowned. "What do you mean?"

"She has you."

He smirked. "I'm like an older brother to her. No more than that."

"Yes, but probably more like family than most. Given that you've been working on the farm for so long. Speaking of which, what do you think of the Donnels?"

"Bunch of…" He seemed to catch himself. "They aren't good people. I warned them to stay away from Belinda and the farm. If you see them here, will you let me know? In fact, I have a friend who works security. Maybe I could have him check up on her."

"Actually, as of last night, I believe they are going to post an officer at the door. That is until the murderer is found."

I was surprised that hadn't happened yet. I understood, though, that Kieran's office was understaffed because of the flu. It was probably one of the reasons there were so many people at the hospital. The few times we'd been here to visit people in the past it had been like a ghost town.

"Do you think the Donnels would go so far as to hurt the Flynns to get them out of the way?"

Joseph snorted. "They are a daft bunch. But I can't see them killing someone. None of them are bright enough to get away with it."

It might be stating the obvious, but he had no love for that family. "Not even for the land?"

He shrugged. "Who knows? I'm not saying it isn't possible.

Old man Donnel is a greedy... man. Over the last few years, he's made more than one offer for the Flynn land. But Mr. Flynn always turned him down, even though it is Belinda who runs the farm now and Declan runs the store."

"I'd forgotten that information."

He nodded. "When he reached seventy, he gave the farm—sans a few acres for me—to our Belinda. And the store was to go to Declan."

"And the family was happy with that arrangement?"

"They were. Mr. Flynn liked the idea of being free so he could just make his clocks and fix things. He didn't want to have to do the books or keep up with things. So, his children took over. Belinda has taken it quite seriously. You would be amazed by how much money she's brought in since taking over. Mainly, with the caravan park and glamping sites. Something none of us saw coming. She'll never sell. She was born on that land, and it is in her blood."

It sounded like it might be in his as well.

It was our turn in the line, so we ordered.

A few minutes later, we carried the four cups down the hall.

We were stopped by Sheila at the door to the hospital room. "I know you're on the list," she said to me. "And you would be?"

"Joseph," he said. "I work on the family farm."

"He's welcome," Belinda said from inside the room. "I put him on the list of family."

That made him smile. He went inside.

"What happened to the officer who was supposed to be posted here yesterday?" I asked Sheila.

"Like everyone else, flu. It's why I'm wearing a mask and gloves. He lasted a few hours and went home with a fever. Everyone else was caught up on other cases."

I nodded. "It's good of you to help out like this."

"What? Because it's beneath me?" She grinned.

"You are second in charge."

"When you work for a station as small as ours, we all have to chip in during hard times."

"Well, thank you for protecting them. They are so vulnerable right now."

She nodded. "Whoever has done all of this deserves a good bangin' on the head."

"I don't disagree. At least, let me get you a chair," I said.

"Now, that, I wouldn't mind. Going to be a long shift."

I asked Belinda if I could take one of the extra wooden chairs in the room and she nodded.

I put it outside the door for Sheila. "You are a doll," she said.

"I do what I can to help local law enforcement."

We laughed.

"That you do," she said. "Though, not sure the boss always sees it that way."

We laughed again.

When I went back in, my sister was saying her goodbyes.

Darn. I'd been hoping to have a chance to speak to Belinda, but Lizzie winked over her shoulder. That meant she had information for me.

"I mean what I said." Lizzie hugged Belinda. "If you need a break, you come around to ours. You can use our guest room to shower and get more than a catnap. You need rest to be strong for your dad."

"Thank you. I may give you a call. And thank you for the food and gifts. You are both too kind."

"Nonsense. Just looking after our friends."

After waving goodbye, I followed Lizzie out to the hallway.

"Wait until we are outside," she whispered.

I nodded.

The rain had started again, and we pulled up our hoods.

"So, what did you find out?"

"She knew nothing about Declan and Jessie," she said. "Like she was stunned when I told her. But she did say he had been secretive and taking a lot of short trips. She thought it had something to do with the shop. But now, she thinks he might have been meeting Jessie. She begged me not to say anything in front of her father, even though he's in a coma. She thinks it would cause him further harm.

"The feud between the Flynns and Simmonses is years old. She said her dad was equally culpable for the stunts each of them had pulled during the years. In many ways, she was embarrassed by the whole thing. She thought they acted like children. But it was her brother's problem as it was to do with the store and not the farm, and she stayed out of it."

"Like what kind of stunts?"

"Dueling ads in the newspaper and all kinds of sales pitches in their window, sometimes denigrating the other store. And then yelling at each other in public places. Last time the police had to separate them in the pub. After their last altercation, Matt banned them from the pub for a month."

I smiled. They did sound like children.

"What else did you find out? Did you ask about the Donnels?"

"I didn't," she said.

Bummer.

"But she brought it up. She wondered if the police were looking into them. They've had some problems at the farm. Small bits of vandalism sort of things. Nothing that they would call the police over, though she's thought about it a few times. Once, they put a rat in the hot tub at the glamping site. But they didn't have any proof that it was the Donnels doing it."

"Did she mention about them wanting to buy the farm?"

She nodded. "Said it would never happen. But I asked her who might want to hurt her family like this. And she said first on her list was them."

"Hmmm."

"What?"

"When I asked Joseph, he seemed to think the Donnels weren't bright enough to plan something like this. He couldn't see them doing it."

"Well, she said either them or Mr. Simmons. I can't tell you how shocked she was about her brother and Jessie. She kept asking, 'Are you sure?'"

"You're the one who always says the heart wants who the heart wants."

"Big cliché you'd never use in your books."

"I don't have a lot of romance in my novels."

"True." She smiled.

"Thank you," I said.

She laughed. "You're not the only one who is mad enough to find whoever is doing this. I'm angry. They are such a sweet family. I don't like it when bad things happen to good people."

"They are good people."

"Do you really think it could be Mr. Simmons?" she asked.

I sighed. "I really don't know. What I can't figure out is why now? What has changed that someone would attack their family? I feel like if we can figure out that answer, the rest will fall into place."

"I think you call that motive," she joked.

"Smarty," I said.

"Everything with Belinda's dad has brought back all those old feelings with Mom. And the hospital. I don't think that smell will ever leave my brain."

I reached around and hugged her. I'd learned she needed those, even if I wasn't much of a hugger. I would do whatever it took to comfort my sister.

"I'm right there with you."

We stopped at the corner that led to our home.

"I need to text Kieran and tell him what we've found. Are you good to go on to the shop alone?"

"Of course. Perhaps it would be good for you to do a bit of writing. How far along are you in the book?"

I snorted. "Has Carrie been texting you again?"

"Maybe. She was checking on me, but wanted to know how things were going with you."

I smirked. "More like snooping."

"I think that is a pot calling the kettle situation."

We laughed.

And then I had that sense that someone might be watching. I turned around quickly, but I didn't see anyone. Then I checked up and down Main Street.

"What is it?" she asked.

"Someone is watching us."

FOURTEEN

Protecting my sister from our stalker was my number one priority. The best way to do that was to head to a public place. "Let's go to the store," I said, and then crooked my arm in hers to pull her along.

"Are we safe?" she whispered.

"I don't know." I had to be honest with her. I would never sugarcoat anything again if her safety depended on it.

"Do you think it has to do with the case?" she said, slightly winded from our fast pace.

"Or it could be our father. I called out to whomever it is the other night. If it is him, he didn't answer. I find it odd that he would continue to keep his distance if he understands we know about him."

"We think we do," she corrected. "There were no real records, and the blood samples disappeared from the hospital. We only think it was him. It could be someone trying to fool us."

"Since when are you the practical one?"

She smiled. "Since always."

Once we were inside the door, we stopped to catch our

breath. Then I turned to stare out the window. No one was there.

Caro stared at us like we'd lost our minds. "Is everything all right?"

My sister hung up her jacket on the coat rack. "We think someone was following us," she said.

Caro raced to the window to look out. Her speed caused Mr. Poe to bark in alarm.

"Can you see who it is?" she asked.

I continued to stare through the glass. I'd learned long ago to trust my instincts. Someone had been there. After waiting for a full two minutes, I popped my head out the door.

There were a few people walking around but none of them were watching the store.

"Is anyone there?" Lizzie and Caro whispered at the same time.

"No. But there was. Promise me you won't go anywhere alone until we find out what is going on," I said.

"I won't allow it," Caro said. "She won't be leavin' without me. I'll walk her home tonight."

My sister and I grinned. Like our friends on the court, Caro had become more like family.

"Thank you," I said.

"Oh, I nearly forgot," Caro whispered. "You said to let you know if Jessie Simmons showed up. She's upstairs." She pointed to the second floor of the shop.

That was a bonus. We'd been trying to find a way to talk to her alone.

"You or me?" my sister asked.

"You know her better. Just be gentle, well, you always are. But you know what I mean."

She nodded. "You go home and write. I'll watch as you go to the secret door. You shouldn't be running around alone either. Take Mr. Poe with you. He could probably use a good trot in the garden once the rain stops. Besides, he'll keep you safe."

I grinned. He might lick an intruder to death, but he wouldn't hurt them. Though he would bark if anyone new tried to come inside the house. And one time he'd latched onto a bad man's pant leg to distract him.

Caro handed me his lead.

I hooked him up. True to her word, Lizzie watched as we made our way down the back alley to the secret stone door on the court. Before pushing through, I waved at her. I wasn't watching where I was going and bumped into a body.

We jumped apart.

"So sorry," Brenna said. "I was glancing back at my place. I think I left my camera on the table. I heard about what happened at yours, and I need to remember to lock my doors."

"It's okay. I wasn't looking either. And I know you all aren't used to it, but locking doors is a good idea for single women. Where were you headed?" She held a plant in her arms.

"To the hospital. I'm up for my part of the schedule. I don't mind though. That Belinda is just lovely. Even though I just met her, I feel like we've been friends forever."

Mr. Poe groaned. He didn't like standing in the rain. He normally wore a little jacket that kept everything but his paws dry.

"I won't keep you," I said. "But I'd love to chat later. If you hear anything that might help with our case, I'd be grateful."

"I'll stop by if I hear anything. And I'll think about my conversations with her. As far as I can remember, things we've talked about didn't involve her dad or brother. Well, except to say she was heartbroken over both."

"Do you by chance know if she's dating anyone?" I thought it might be Joseph, but they seemed more like family.

"It hasn't come up," she said. "But I'll try to find a way to ask. She's a crafter, so we talked a bit about knitting. I've just started." She pointed to the huge bag on her shoulder. "She was going to show me some stitches. I thought it might help pass the time."

"That's kind of you," I said. "I love our little neighborhood. Everyone is so good at looking after others."

"They are. Including you and Lizzie."

My sister was better at it than I was, but I had grown closer to these people than any of my neighbors in New York. Who was I kidding? I didn't know a single person in my building back there, other than the doormen who worked the front desk. I was still getting used to that—everyone knowing my business.

"Well, don't force the issue but if she does mention someone or anyone with the last name Donnel, let me know."

She grinned.

"What?"

"I never really get to be involved in your investigations. You have helped me so many times. I'm happy to do you a favor. Oh, you are coming to the fête, aren't you? We had another meeting this afternoon. It's going to be so much fun."

"I plan on it. My sister is excited about what you all have planned."

"She's so creative. This will be our best year yet. And it brings in so many visitors for the shops and businesses. I always feel like a kid that first day."

"It sounds like fun."

"I should get going. But I won't forget to let you know if I hear anything."

"Thanks," I said as she walked off.

I waved and Mr. Poe and I headed home. After unlocking the door, he ran inside and sat on the mat. We had a routine when it was wet outside, which was often. He sat on the mat, and we wrapped him in a big fluffy towel that we kept by the door.

I put my things down on the hall table and picked up the

towel. After wrapping him up like a baby. I rubbed his fur dry. When I let him down, he shook his whole body like his life depended on it.

I laughed. "I need a coffee, and then I have to do some writing."

He grumbled but followed me to the kitchen. I checked to make certain his bowl had clean water. His food bowl had to be presented precisely at five in the evening. If we were more than a minute late, there would be more grumbling and grunting.

I had a feeling my sister had been feeding him one too many treats—even though she kept saying we shouldn't—which was probably why he preferred her. Though, I really was no better.

After making a cortado, and grabbing a muffin my sister had made, we headed to my office.

I flipped the switch that turned the fire on and Mr. Poe climbed into his bed situated in front of it.

After writing everything I'd learned in my notebook, I also wrote down the times when it felt like someone had been watching us on the street. When I next managed to speak with Kieran, I'd ask if he could check the CCTV.

I finished writing my notes, and then I turned my attention to my book. The next thing I knew, it was several hours later, and Mr. Poe sat next to my chair. He grunted a few times, which was his signal for a bathroom break.

"Come on," I said. "I could use a stretch."

I was surprised to see the sun had come out, though every-thing was still very wet. While I leaned on the banister of the deck we'd had put in, he chased birds away from the fountain. For some reason, he considered any creature an intruder in *his* garden.

Normally, I'd complain about the barking, but at least he was getting some exercise, which was good for him.

I closed my eyes and breathed in the fresh air. The air was one of my favorite things about our new place. There was no pollution. And I spent more time taking walks and hikes than I ever had in my life. I tried not to think of it as exercise. More like an exploration of our new home.

Mr. Poe grumbled by my feet. I opened my eyes and smiled down at him.

"What now?"

He grunted.

I glanced at my watch. "Oh. I see. You're right. Come on then."

I scooped out his food and put it in his bowl. He sat politely glancing from me to the bowl.

"Go ahead," I said.

He dived into his kibble.

My phone dinged. It was a message from Kieran.

Caught up on another case. Tomorrow interviews. 11 a.m.

I had no idea who he meant by the interviews. I texted back:

Interview who? And are you asking me to come with?

Donnels and yes.

He'd said that he didn't want me there before. I wondered what had changed. Though I'd never argue. Keeping me in the loop was a new thing and I was grateful. He was right, it meant I didn't have to go off alone putting myself in possible danger.

It sounded like he was busy, or I would have asked him to check the CCTV, but that could wait. At least, until tomorrow morning. His staff was stretched thin as it was.

I felt like I should be doing more. There was more than one suspect. The Donnels, Mr. Simmons, Jessie Simmons, and then... Wait. Something hit my brain like a freight train. So many of the facts about the attack and murder didn't add up.

If Declan Flynn took the items from the store, why break in or hurt his father? He had keys. And then, why hide them on his boat? Though they could have been planted there. We hadn't talked about that.

Then who murdered Declan Flynn, and why? We were no closer to an answer. It was frustrating.

But my brain shouted: What if it is two separate crimes? Meaning two suspects.

I'd done that in more than one novel. It helped confuse my detective.

What if the same thing had happened here?

If I separated the crimes. Perhaps Declan Flynn made it look like a break-in to get the insurance money. It didn't explain why he would hurt his father though. A man he obviously loved.

Unless Mr. Flynn senior stumbled onto the scene. And what if Declan had hired someone who messed up?

That same someone could have killed him. Or that might be a completely different crime. Murder was a far reach from stealing. If Declan did have a partner, they could have turned on him, yes. Or with both the Flynn men out of pocket, that would make it easier for the criminals to get their hands on either the business, or the farm. Perhaps both.

What if the Donnels and Mr. Simmons were working together?

I snorted. That was a bit of a reach. I didn't even know if they were aware of one another.

I remembered that Lizzie was supposed to have spoken with Jessie.

I pulled out my phone again and texted her.

Any news from your customer?

She didn't answer at first.

"Probably busy."

A few minutes later, I sat down at the table munching on another muffin. I could use a real meal. I thought about seeing if she wanted to go to the pub tonight. I always felt guilty that she was the only one who cooked. Though I'd become a pro at cleaning up.

Sometimes I liked to treat us to a night out.

I'd just picked up the mess I made with the muffin when my phone dinged.

Too much info to text. Be home soon. You won't believe what I found out.

Great.

Way to keep me hanging, sis.

FIFTEEN

While it was only a half-hour wait, it felt more like a day until my sister came in the door. But she didn't come alone. Caro was with her. They came straight to the kitchen. Mr. Poe was happy to see them and as soon as my sister sat down, he jumped up in her lap.

"Okay, now that she's home safe, I'm off. I have a date," Caro said.

"A date?" That was new. Caro had sworn off men as of a few months ago. Her last boyfriend had been married. She found out in the worst way.

"Yes. Don't worry. He's been thoroughly vetted by my ma. He goes to her church. And she knows his ma. So, if he doesn't act right, the whole church will know. I'll tell you about it tomorrow." She was fifteen years our senior but had a far more active social life than the two of us combined.

She gave my sister a quick squeeze and walked out.

"That was sweet of her to walk you home."

"She insisted. Kieran came by earlier and mentioned for our safety that we shouldn't go around town alone."

"He did?"

"Yes." She frowned. "He said that he'd already spoken to you about it. I told him you had said something to me as well. But Caro is a bit of a mother hen. She worries."

"That she does. So, tell me what you found out from Jessie?"

"Oh. I thought you would want to go eat first. I'm starving."

"Let's chat on the way. The pub will be crowded."

She still had her coat on, and I grabbed mine. After putting on Mr. Poe's raincoat harness, we headed out.

We opened the secret door slowly and I peeked up and down the alleyway. No one was there. As we made our way to the corner to cross over to Main Street there were a few people out and about, but it was a weekend night.

"Okay, tell me what happened," I said softly.

"Right. So, I quickly went upstairs after you left the store and it looked like Jessie had been crying—a lot. I found her in the corner of the kids' section holding a book of Thomas Moore poems."

"And?"

"When I asked if she was all right, words just spilled out. And I sat with her. She told me that Thomas Moore's *A Dream of Turtle* was Declan's favorite poem. He never explained why. She felt bad that she'd never asked him."

My sister had her own way of telling a story. Interrupting her would only mean starting over. So I tried to be patient.

"I asked if they were close, and she sobbed even harder. Then she told me they'd gone to Dublin to get married. They had a license and everything. It was supposed to happen today. But Jessie got a message from a friend about his dad—Declan had lost his phone—and he came back. She's heartbroken. Says if they had just stayed away, they would be on their honeymoon."

"Surely she understands why he had to come back since his dad was attacked?"

"Of course, but you get it. She's a young bride, whose dreams are dashed. She's heartbroken that her man was killed."

"Only someone from Texas would say it that way," I said.

"Well, it's true. Anyway, she's had a huge row with her dad. She came into the bookstore to take her mind off her troubles."

"Did she have any idea who might have hurt the Flynns?"

"That's the thing. I tried to ask her delicately, she said no, at first. But then she said it could have been the Donnels. They had been arguing with the Flynns over some land."

That was new. 'Some land' wasn't buying them out, which was what we'd been told before.

"I asked about her dad, gently, mind you. Said he would be angry when he found out the truth. And would have been furious about their marriage. But she promised he would have come to terms with it eventually. She did say Declan had been acting weirdly the last few weeks. She thought it was because they were making a big decision, but now she isn't so certain."

Strange behavior was usually a sign of something more serious. "He could have been seeing someone else. It wouldn't be unusual for a man, or woman, to want to sow a few oats before marrying. Or so I've heard."

"That is so wrong, and way too logical. I mean, I get that is what the stag and hen parties are for that they have here. But to cheat? You met him. Did you think he could do that to Jessie?"

"I didn't know him. He was a nice guy who loved his dad. I can't tell you much more than that. And people seldom surprise me. After writing so many novels, I've come to expect all kinds of unexpected behaviors."

"I didn't know them," she said. "Personally, I mean. I knew of them."

"You didn't mention the stolen items being found in his boat, did you? I think Kieran wants that kept a secret for now."

Lizzie stopped. "Did you tell me that? Don't worry. I didn't say anything because I didn't remember that."

Sometimes I forgot what Kieran and I had shared versus what I told my sister. My memory was usually better—unless I was working on a book, which I was. I had too many characters and plot twists rolling around in there. Sometimes I didn't have room for anything else. That was why I wrote everything down in my trusty notebook.

"We definitely need to tell Kieran about the strange behavior. He'll need to get more in depth about that. Maybe Declan owed someone money or something. I keep thinking the robbery was an insurance scam. He hires someone to break in, probably thinking his dad would go home to the farm. But then his dad catches the person, and he or she attacks Mr. Flynn."

"That makes sense to me. But then why kill Declan?"

It was too early to share my idea that it might be two separate criminals. "That I don't have an answer to. Since the items were stored on the boat, could be possible he was going to try and fence them later."

"Honeymoons aren't cheap," she said.

"Do you know where they had been heading?"

"Maldives, I think. She said it was their dream trip. That they'd even talked about never coming back so they didn't have to deal with their family. But she says they would have. He loved his family, and she loves her dad. They would have come back and faced them, eventually.

"But then she started bawling again. I gave her a cup of tea and a muffin. She bought a few books and then went on her way."

"I'll text Kieran. By the way, you did great. You're getting good at investigating."

"I prefer to call it caring about people."

We laughed.

"Potato, potato."

"You said that the same way twice."

"Exactly."

She snorted.

As we came to the pub door, I pulled it open and let her and Mr. Poe inside.

"Ah, it's our favorite twins and the best dog in the world," Matt called across the pub.

Mr. Poe barked, and everyone in the pub laughed.

"Your table is available in the back, be there in a bit. Pints?"

We nodded.

After we sat down, Lizzie put Mr. Poe in the chair next to her. He curled up as if he knew she would be feeding him soon.

"Matt knows everything about everyone," she whispered. "You should ask him about your suspects."

Matt flitted from one table to another.

"Not a bad idea, but he looks busy."

She glanced behind her. "He does. Still. He is one of our best resources for information."

"True."

He brought our pints, and one of the printed menus. He knelt, which put him on the same level with us. He was quite tall and one of the kindest men we'd met in Shamrock Cove. That was saying something since kindness was a thing here.

"You two here for dinner or information?" he whispered. Usually, anything said in the pub was around town before one left the place.

"I have no idea what you mean," I whispered back and then smiled.

He laughed. "What do you need to know?"

"So many things," I said.

"Tough case?"

I nodded.

He glanced around. "Ask away."

The two tables around us had just emptied. That gave us a bit of privacy, but it wouldn't last long.

"Have you heard anything about the Flynns?"

"That's a bad business. They were both good men. I mean that. Younger one sometimes had a few too many and we had to get him a ride home. But that happens a lot around here. His da is the best. He looked out for all of us."

He sighed.

"What is it?"

"When I was in school, sometimes I was bullied. Mr. Flynn caught some boys chasing me down the street one day. Called their parents and made them apologize. I didn't have any trouble after that. Being gay in a small town wasn't always easy."

"I don't think it is easy anywhere these days," I said.

"You make a good point."

"What else can you tell us? Anyone who might wish them harm?"

"Simmons. Loudmouth and a jerk to everyone. I don't know how he makes money. No one can stand him. His daughter is good people. She was sweet on Declan. Caught them giving each other the eye when they were here the last few months. Can't imagine that would have gone over well with her da."

We'd all been thinking the same thing.

"Anything else?"

"Let me grab you some food and I'll have a think. I'm guessing you want the specials?"

We had no idea what those were, but we trusted him. My sister and I glanced at each other and then nodded.

He stood and had gone a few steps and came back. "Declan was in here with a guy I'd never seen before. It was a few weeks ago. Something about the guy didn't feel right. I know that doesn't help, but as a bartender and barista, we learn to pick up on things."

"Any chance you could give a description of him? Maybe to Sheila?"

He grinned. "Never forget a face."

"Excellent. I knew we could count on you."

"I'll ask Ma if she's heard anything."

"Thank you."

"We do what we can. Isn't that what you two always say?"

"It is," Lizzie said. "Was Mr. Flynn senior in recently? Did you see him with anyone?"

He put his hand on his chin. "He met up with Petey a few times a week to play chess. Come to think of it, Petey hasn't been in for a few days." He frowned.

"What is it?"

"We're Petey's main source of meals. I wonder if he's sick?"

"Why don't I have Kieran do a welfare check." I looked at my sister. "Or we could take him some food over—after we eat, we could go check on him. Do you know where he lives?"

"I do. I'll put a care package together for him. I learned that phrase from Lizzie. I'll make a good American yet."

"No. Never leave us, Matt. This town couldn't live without your coffee or pints."

He laughed. "There is that. I'm not going anywhere anytime soon. Two specials coming up."

By the time we left, an hour later, we had sacks of food for Petey.

"Do you know him?" I asked, as we walked down Main Street.

"Petey? Yes. He likes historical fiction and anything to do with the seventeen hundreds."

I smiled. "So, he's a customer at the store?"

"He comes in a few times a month and looks through our inventory. I've even special-ordered a few items for him. He's quiet. Likes chess and was in the army when he was younger."

"Seems like you know quite a bit," I said.

"You've met me. I like to get to know our clients. Caro said he was married years ago. His wife died and he split his time between the bookstore and the pub. He and Grandad were friends."

"Oh?" I was always hungry for information about Driscoll O'Heyne, our grandfather who we never knew. It was because of him we were here. He'd left us his home and bookstore.

"Did he have stories?"

She sighed. "A few, but usually how Grandad gave him a good discount."

I laughed.

"He's a sweet old guy," she said. "Lonely, for certain. And I appreciate his taste in books."

"Do you think he'll mind that we are bringing him food? Or that I want to ask him questions?"

"Depends on his mood. I think the food might help."

He lived a few blocks away from the hospital, which was a bit of a trek. Since we'd both had slices of pie, and two bowls of Guinness stew, we needed to walk off the carbs.

My sister checked her phone where Matt had typed in the address.

The house was a thatched cottage, much like ours, though this one was painted brown with white trim. The garden in the front wasn't fancy, but it was clean and well-cared for, as was the house.

My sister knocked on the door.

No one answered. She frowned and looked back at me.

She knocked again. We heard some movement inside, but the door still wasn't answered.

What was going on? I started to worry that Petey might be in trouble.

"Petey, it's Lizzie from the bookstore. I have some food from the pub. Matt and his mom sent it to you. They were worried maybe you weren't feeling well."

A few minutes later, the door opened. A stooped elderly

gentleman stood before them wearing a knit cap, a sweater and jeans. It was dark, but he didn't look well.

"Lizzie?" He seemed more surprised than upset. "What are you doing here?"

She held up the bags of food. "Matt and his mom hadn't seen you at the pub. They thought you might be hungry." Her voice was soft and kind. She really had a way with people.

"You better come inside then." He walked away and we followed him to the back of the house. The kitchen light was on. It appeared not much had changed since the late seventies, but it was clean and neat. "I'll put the kettle on," he said.

We'd learned that was how Irish people mostly said welcome.

"You don't need to go to any trouble. Are you feeling okay?"

He shrugged. "Had the flu, but I'm better now."

We set the food on the counter and Lizzie pulled out a few containers. "I have stew and pie," she said. "All courtesy of the Crown and Clover."

He sat down at an old fiberglass table. It reminded me of something out of a fifties diner. "That was kind of them."

He pointed at me. "You the famous writer?"

I smiled. "I'm a writer," I said. "I don't know about famous."

He grunted. "You're famous. Your grandfather was proud of you both. Talked about your success and your sister's."

Hearing that made my cold, black heart swell with pride. I wished he would have introduced himself to us before he died. But he'd been being kind. We were going through so much loss and, at the time, he didn't want to add to it.

"Do we need to take you to the hospital?" Lizzie said as she put a bowl of the stew in front of him. "You're looking pale, Petey."

"I'll be fine. Saw the doc earlier in the week. Just a bit on the tired side now. I'm healthy as can be at my age."

"Have you gone to visit your friend at the hospital?" I asked.

"Mr. Flynn was so kind to me. I can't believe someone attacked him."

"They should be strung up for hurting an old man. No sense in it. He didn't have much. Just his precious clocks."

"I agree," Lizzie said. "It makes me so mad. You know Mercy was the one who found him. Well, and Mr. Poe here."

He grinned and leaned down to pet our dog. "Been missing you, little fella."

"Are you certain you don't need to go back to the doctor?" Lizzie said.

"I'm just sad, girlie. A grown man shouldn't admit that. Haven't felt like eating. Flynn is my last friend." He sniffed.

My eyes watered and I glanced down at my shoes. I hadn't expected him to be so honest.

Lizzie wrapped her arms around him and squeezed him. "I'm so sorry," she said. "But he's not gone yet. We should stay hopeful."

"Saw him tonight. It doesn't look good. Never seen him so quiet." He laughed but it wasn't a happy sound. "Thought he was a decent chess player. I'm better, of course."

"Of course you are," she said. "Mercy plays a pretty mean game, though I doubt she could keep up with you."

That made him smile. "Without my chess mate, not much reason to head to the pub."

"Except you need to eat," she said.

"Just didn't have the energy to walk down there."

"Well, I'm going to leave our number with you. Any time you need a ride, you just call. I mean it."

"You don't need to rush off, do you?" he asked.

"No," we said at the same time. "Actually, I'm helping the police with their inquiries. Do you know of anyone who would hurt the family?"

He sighed. "Always had trouble with those pesky Donnels. But I can't see any of them being bright enough to plan a crime.

I heard the break-in might be kids. We haven't had trouble like that in some time."

"And what about Declan?"

"That boy has always been trouble, but nothing worth murdering over. If my friend wakes up, he's going to be crushed about his boy. Seemed like the young man was finally getting his life together."

I leaned my elbows on the table while he took a few sips of the stew. The color began to come back into his cheeks.

"Can I ask what kind of trouble Declan was in?"

"Nothing much. He'd get caught up in schemes trying to make fast money. His da tried his best to teach him that you had to work for your money. I thought the boy had finally learned his lesson. But they'd been having arguments again. Flynn wouldn't tell me why."

"Oh?" Lizzie and I said it at the same time. It was a twin thing. We could also finish each other's sentences, but we didn't. It was annoying to others.

"Mr. Flynn was talking about expanding the farm again. Declan kept trying to bully his sister and my friend wasn't having it. That Belinda has a good head on her shoulders. She knows what she's doing."

"Were the brother and sister arguing? I thought she was into expanding her business."

"She is, but it was what he wanted to do. He wanted investors and to partner with someone to create a resort. She wanted to keep it in the family. I don't know all the particulars. You'll have to ask Belinda."

I would do exactly that. Funny how she hadn't mentioned any of that during our visits. Though, when our loved ones died, we sometimes forgot the stressful times and focused on the good.

She'd been so upset about her brother. But could she be a suspect? Or maybe it was someone close to her?

SIXTEEN

By the time we left Petey's we were all exhausted, including Mr. Poe. I still hadn't heard back from Kieran, but if he was busy with another case that made sense. Besides, we were set to meet the next morning.

"I feel sorry for him," Lizzie said.

"Who? Petey?"

"He's frightened that he is about to lose his best friend. Maybe, I should do an older person's book club. That would give those in the village who can't get out as much a chance to visit with one another."

My sister was always thinking about others, sometimes to her detriment but it was one of the things I loved most about her. That heart of hers was big enough for the both of us.

"Perhaps you could suggest larger print books for the reading list," I said.

"That's a great idea. I bet Lolly and her friends would join the fun."

"I thought they already had their book club."

She laughed. "You've met Lolly. Any chance to have a party."

"True."

As we turned the corner onto Main Street, I had that weird feeling again.

I paused. Then Mr. Poe barked. He must have heard or seen something.

Lizzie stopped and glanced up and down the street. "What's wrong?" she whispered.

"Someone is watching us again," I said.

"Whoever you are, we know you're there. Don't be a coward." I was angry. And tired of all of this.

Mr. Poe barked as if to back me up. I turned in circles trying to find whoever it was, but then that sense was gone.

"Are we okay?" Lizzie asked.

"Yes. Come on. Let's go home."

Mr. Poe seemed to agree as he pulled on his leash.

"Who do you think it is? Is it case related?"

"I wish I knew."

"Is it..."

I understood who she meant. We'd been wondering if the man from the hospital, the one who had been hit by a car, had been our father. Unfortunately, by the time we'd found out about the accident he was gone. And strangely none of the security cameras had been working. There had been terrible storms, and the backup generators were routed only to necessities, like keeping people alive.

And he'd taken the paper chart with him when he left. The name given wasn't our father's, but the description the nurses gave us... we were certain it was him. We'd thought him dead in some war he'd been fighting long ago. So had our grandfather.

What I didn't understand was why, if it really was him, he didn't just come forward?

As we walked down Main Street the tightness in my chest loosened. Whoever had been watching us was gone.

Then there was a loud noise, as some huge trucks passed by. We jumped.

"Oh, wow. I forgot about that starting soon," I said.

The trucks carried carnival rides and there were several huge box trucks. The summer fête was set to begin in a few days. The rides and carnival booths would be set up on the cliffs and jetty by the sea.

"With the summer fête opening, I expect we'll have a bit more traffic the next few weeks," she said. "It's our first summer at the store. Lolly said we do a good tourist trade here. Hopefully, that will be good for sales."

"People always need a beach read," I said.

"Oh, that reminds me, I should do a window display for exactly that," she said.

"It's a great idea."

Another truck went by with what looked like a third of a Ferris wheel.

"Does it make me immature that I want to ride everything they have?" I asked.

"Well, if it does, that makes two of us."

"I wonder if they'll have one of those things where you stick to the side and the floor gives way." I smiled.

"You just want to see if I'll puke again. It wasn't my fault."

"Kind of was," I said. "You ate four funnel cakes that day."

She laughed. "True."

We turned the corner and headed down the alley to the secret door. Only pausing to look both ways before we pushed through into our little bailey of the castle.

"This is a reminder that we don't go anywhere alone," I said.

"Agreed. That goes for you as well," my sister pointed out.

"Right."

"Wait," I whispered. "Someone is on our porch." We'd

forgotten to turn on the light, which we usually did at dusk every night. And I had no weapon. "I don't know who you are, but you better get away from our door." I sounded far braver than I felt.

"Get ready to run to Rob and Scott's," I whispered.

"It's me," Kieran called out. "I tried to text to let you know I was coming by, but you didn't answer."

I'd turned the sound off on my phone when I'd been writing earlier and had forgotten to turn it back on. Typical me.

We passed through our garden gate. Mr. Poe tore out of Lizzie's hand and ran for the detective inspector.

Kieran scooped him up. "You're wet, little fella." Mr. Poe licked his chin. "Okay, okay. I guess after the day I had, a little wet dog is no problem."

I unlocked the door.

"You might as well come in," my sister said. Then she took Mr. Poe and grabbed the towel we kept by the door to dry him off.

"I know it's late."

"It is," she said. "But my sister has a lot to tell you. There are cookies in the kitchen jar. Mr. Poe and I are going to bed." She waved us off.

I grinned. She was tired and I was excited to see Kieran. And it wasn't just because I had a lot to tell him. I'd grown to enjoy his company more than I wanted to admit to myself.

"Come on back," I said.

"Are you certain it's okay? I can come back tomorrow if you're tired."

"No. It's fine. Really. I'm glad you stopped by." I was tired, but I wouldn't be able to sleep until I told him everything my sister and I had learned.

We made some coffees, decaf for me. He had the rest of his shift to get through, so he took his fully loaded.

Then we sat down with a plate of cookies, and I told him all I had learned.

"So, everything isn't as it looks where the sister is concerned."

"But I've spent some time with her. I can't imagine her doing anything to harm her family. She appears truly devastated by the loss of her brother and she hasn't left her dad's bedside."

"You're right. I can't see her doing anything like this. But that doesn't mean she's off the suspect list. We have to keep an eye on everyone."

"Have you searched the apartment upstairs from the shop?"

"My team did a thorough search. Why?"

"I don't know about you, but I'd feel better if you and I took a quick look. Nothing against your team but something that seems innocuous to them, could be a lead. At least, now that we know a bit more about the family."

He raised his eyebrows but nodded. "When do you want to do that?"

"You said you wanted to talk to the Donnels tomorrow morning. We could check the apartment before that. And maybe go through his room at the farm again?"

"As you know, I already have search warrants for both places. Even though Belinda gave us permission and keys, I wanted to keep everything by the book."

I grinned. "That's always a good idea."

"Yes, but you and by the book aren't always in line." He smiled and something fluttered in my stomach. He really was just looking out for me.

I laughed. "True. You said there was another case today. Anything I can help you with?"

"No. Property dispute between the Donnels and the Flynns. A bunch of hotheads with no sense."

"What were they arguing about exactly?"

"The Donnels are saying the new fence the Flynns put up is three inches onto their property. Nothing to be done about it until we can get copies of the property evaluations and deeds."

"It seems like the Donnels are always arguing with someone about their land. I heard a rumor that they weren't—" I stopped.

"What?"

"It wasn't nice, and I shouldn't repeat it. But maybe that they were a bit, um, hard-headed."

He laughed. "That is one way of putting it. They've always been a rowdy bunch. In and out of trouble, especially the younger ones in the family. Some have spent time in prison in Dublin."

"They sound like the perfect murder suspects," I said. "They had a beef with the Flynn family."

"I'm lacking proof," he said. "They all have alibis, though some of them are for one another. So, they are not exactly in the clear. The father and sons happened to be in the Crown and Clover that night for the pub quiz. Then they stayed to play darts."

"But do you have CCTV proof? That reminds me."

"What?"

"You know I told you I keep feeling like someone might be watching me and my sister?"

He frowned. "Yes. What's going on?" He sounded genuinely worried, and I appreciated that he took me seriously.

"Can you check some dates and times for me on Main Street?" I pulled out my notebook and showed him each time I'd felt someone might be watching.

"Why didn't you tell me?"

"I did, but maybe not every time." I explained about when we'd been walking home. "And before you yell, we've been careful about only going out when someone can be with us," I said.

"I never yell."

I may have snorted.

"It's not in my nature." His eyebrows went up, and then we grinned.

"I'll see what we can grab from CCTV. Text me the date and times."

"Thanks."

"So, give me your rundown as to where you think the case is going," he said.

"My main suspect is Mr. Simmons. If he found out about his daughter and Declan... he wouldn't have been happy. He and Mr. Flynn senior could have argued. But then why did the stolen goods end up on the Flynns' boat?"

"Good question," he said.

"I haven't met the Donnels. I saw them at the pub that night, but I couldn't tell you if they were all there. I wasn't sure who they were, except they were loud and often rude. Your grandmother wasn't too happy with them. But, like I said, I don't think any of us from the court could tell you if they were there all night. How about you? Have you narrowed down the list of perps?" I asked.

He grinned at my use of the American term. "I'm right there with you, as you like to say. But I'm not sure Declan wasn't trying on some sort of insurance scam. Like you said, why hide the jewelry on the boat?"

"Unless it was someone trying to make him look guilty."

He sighed. "There is that possibility. I heard a few of the Donnels have part-time jobs with the fête. Day laborer type things. We will check with them tomorrow. After you and I go through the elder Mr. Flynn's things."

I smiled.

"What?"

"It's nice to be included."

"We've talked about this. It's only because if I don't, you'll go off and get yourself into trouble. We've played that game before."

He wasn't wrong. But there were times when a police presence wasn't welcome. During those moments it was easier for me to be on my own, so that the suspect wasn't worried about Kieran hauling them off to jail for saying the wrong thing.

"What time do you want to head out tomorrow?"

"My shift isn't over until midnight. So, let's say ten, if that works for you. I'll come by and pick you up. We'll hit the apartment first."

"Sounds good. Do you want a coffee to go?"

He cocked his head. "It's like you don't know me."

We laughed.

"Coffee to go coming up."

If I drank the real thing after two or so, I was up all night. Great when I was on a deadline. Other times, not so much.

After he left, I headed to my office. My brain was going ninety to nothing. I felt like, even though it had only been a few days, we should be much closer to a real suspect. There were too many balls in the air.

Real-life mysteries weren't as neatly wrapped up as those in fiction where I could plot every move, throw in a few red herrings, and surprise readers at the end. Even though I'd carefully laid the groundwork for my killer.

If I'd learned anything since dabbling in real-life crimes, it was that the non-fiction world was messy. And it was impossible to believe anyone until that final confession.

The next morning, I set an alarm. When I made my way to the kitchen, my sister was surprised. "Why are you up so early?"

I did tend to sleep late when I was writing. Mainly because I'd fall asleep on my keyboard, which I'd done the night before. I'd set the alarm when Kieran left so I wouldn't forget.

"I'm going to do some sleuthing with Kieran today," I said. I couldn't keep the stupid grin off my face.

"Oh?"

"Don't say it like that. The only reason he asked me along is that he is still short-handed."

"And he doesn't want you to get into trouble on your own." She smirked.

"Whatever," I said. I sounded like a sullen teen. But she wasn't wrong.

"When those carnival trucks went by it reminded me. Can I still count on you to help at our booth at the fête? Our summer help will be coming in, but I have set up a signing for you. If you're running behind on book deadlines, I can cancel though."

"I can do that. No worries. And if Carrie is still bothering you, tell her I said to stop." I loved my editor. She'd become a dear friend, but she had a job to do, and that was keeping me on track.

"It might help if you sent your poor editor an update. Maybe like now. You could give her an idea where you are with things?"

I sighed. "I'm sorry that she bugs you about my deadlines."

She smiled. "I consider her a friend. She looked after both of us when Mom died... and then..." She cleared her throat. It was still hard for her to talk about her fiancé and his daughter. "I don't know what we would have done without her."

"True. And you're right. I'll text her after I get some coffee."

Luckily, I'd been able to get some writing done and I would more than likely make my deadline. Maybe not until the last minute, but it would be emailed to Carrie by the due date. After everything that had happened the past year before we arrived in Shamrock Cove, I was almost caught up. Almost.

I was grateful to my editor and publisher for giving me time to grieve our family. But it turned out moving to Ireland had been the creative boost I needed to get myself back on track.

My sister seemed to be thriving as well, which made me extremely happy.

After eating an apple muffin just out of the oven, and downing my first cup of coffee, I poured two more cups and put three of the muffins in a paper sack my sister kept in one of the drawers.

"Is that for Kieran?"

"He had a late night," I said.

"Right." She grinned.

"We're just friends investigating," I said. Though it felt like we'd passed the friend zone a few months ago. I had no idea what we were. And I wasn't a big fan of labels.

"Uh huh. Because he does that with *all* his friends."

It wasn't the first time she'd alluded to something between the detective inspector and me. "Stop it."

She held up her hands in surrender. "I never said a word. I think it's sweet he's so protective of you. And that he knows you so well."

"What do you mean by that?"

"If he doesn't take you with him, you'll just go off on your own. And possibly get yourself killed. He's very protective these days."

I cleared my throat. "I'll take an extra muffin for me."

"Changing the subject doesn't make the truth any less... well, true." She laughed. "Are you ready to go? We can walk each other to the bookstore. Maybe he can meet you there."

"Smart. I'll text him."

After putting the leash on Mr. Poe, we headed out. It was overcast, but no rain so far. The sun even peeked through now and then as we walked. But I still brought my mac and my umbrella.

When we made it to the back door, I pulled my sister back.

"What is it?"

I pointed to the lock. There were several marks as if someone had tried to jimmy the lock.

She turned to look at me with wide eyes.

"I'm texting Kieran," I said. I did exactly that, and then I stood by the back door with my umbrella poised as a weapon.

SEVENTEEN

Kieran and several of his men showed up. After I pointed out what we'd seen, he sent a few of them to the front of the store.

He silently tried the door, but it was still locked.

Good, maybe the thief never made it inside.

He reached a hand out, and Lizzie gave him the keys.

"Stay," he whispered to us.

I started to follow him in, but my sister pulled me back.

"For once, do what he asked," she said.

"Whoever it is didn't make it inside, or the door wouldn't have been locked."

"Or they are still inside and locked the door. And they could be waiting to murder us."

I grinned. "Now who has the wild imagination?"

She rolled her eyes.

"Come on in and take a look around," he said. "I don't think they made it inside, but I'll have forensics come in and we'll check the office and front door as well. Could be when they tried to get in, they left some prints behind."

"I'm sorry I called you for no reason," I said.

"Don't be. I'm glad you did. It was the smart thing to do."

"She has her moments," Lizzie joked. And then they laughed.

I really wanted to say, whatever, again. But I would only sound like a petulant teen.

"Do you think Lizzie will be safe here?"

He nodded. "They would be stupid to try something during the day. I need to look at the security tapes for the back and front doors."

"Follow me," Lizzie said.

"Use these." He handed her some gloves. And then gave some to me. "We have your fingerprints on file, but it will be faster for us if we are careful."

"Understood," she said. She pulled up the security video for the night before. Kieran and I stood behind her.

"There," I said. I pointed to a hooded figure. It was as if they knew the camera was there. It was dark and raining, and the camera was smeared a bit. Other than the figure was slim and tall, there wasn't much more to tell.

"Go ahead and email that to me," Kieran said. "We can have our techs in Dublin see if they can enhance it in some way."

"Why would someone want to rob us? We don't keep cash in the store. We take it to the bank every evening."

"You have some pretty valuable books though, behind the counter," I said. "Anyone who knows about first editions could try to resell them."

"Or they could have been looking for information," he said. "I'm glad you installed the cameras outside of the store, but you may want to put some inside as well."

"I don't like the idea of spying on customers," she said.

"It can be discreet and can cut down on shoplifting thefts. We don't have much trouble with that, until the out of towners come in, and you can't be too safe."

"Okay. I'll call the company today," she said. "Do I have to keep the store closed? I have two mommy-and-me book clubs coming in today."

I smiled. She really was the best thing that ever happened to this bookstore. Our grandfather had barely kept it running, but a few months in and Lizzie had completely turned it around. She had the golden touch that way.

"The forensics team is already here. It should only take them a few minutes on each of the doors. It doesn't look like the intruder made it inside. But I don't need to remind you to always keep this back door locked. And maybe get a double bolt. The more keys it takes, the better."

"I'll do that when I call the security company. Thank you, Kieran, for everything," she said.

"No need for that. It's my job. My team has things handled here. Mercy, are you ready to go across the street again?"

I leaned down and hugged my sister. "Are you going to be okay?"

She shooed me away. "I'll be fine. I have Mr. Poe, and Caro is due in any minute. Can you let your team know she's okay to come inside?" she asked Kieran.

"Will do."

A few minutes later, we'd crossed the street. The glass door of the clock store was still boarded up. But Kieran used a key to get in. I was still wearing the gloves he'd handed me earlier.

The store had a musty smell, but the blood on the floor had been cleaned up, as had the glass from the cases around the room. The clocks still hung on the wall looking down on us as if we were trespassers.

Well, we were.

"It's so sad. I wonder if someone will take it over," I said.

"I don't know," Kieran said. "From what Belinda told me; she doesn't have much interest with the shop. If Mr. Flynn doesn't pull through..."

"It's just sad how fast a life can be taken. I know there is very little chance he will wake up, but he was so lovely to me and my sister."

"He was one of the good ones. Let's start upstairs." I followed him to the back room where a set of stairs went up to the next floor. They were old and narrow. They creaked as we walked up them.

"Hmmm," I said.

"What?"

"These stairs make so much noise. The intruder would have heard Flynn coming down them. Why wouldn't he or she just run away? Why confront him?"

"If we had that answer, we'd be far closer to the truth," Kieran admitted.

"I'm so annoyed that they attacked an old man. Who does that?"

"Someone who belongs in the jail. But I have new information about that. The doctors at the hospital are certain he had a cardiac event first, and then most likely pitched forward and hit his head on the glass case. The forensics back that up."

"So, he wasn't attacked?"

"That we can't know for certain until we talk to him. But from what the doctors say, he didn't have any other bruising other than the force of gravity from him falling, which is why the damage is so extensive."

"Still, someone may have caused that, and they robbed the store. Then there is poor Declan. If it is the same person."

"We're waiting on DNA results from both scenes. Maybe we'll get lucky. And from what I can tell the inventory shows the store wasn't robbed, except for the items we found on the boat."

"Well, that is interesting. Maybe Declan robbed his own store for insurance?"

"Or he was trying to keep the items safe from someone

else," Kieran said, and then shrugged. "Difficult to know at this point why we found the goods where we did."

"Do you think you'll find the same DNA here as on the boat?"

"I try not to make assumptions. It's best—"

"To follow the evidence," I finished his sentence.

He laughed. "You do listen."

"Hey, I'm the first to admit I've learned a great deal from you. And the first to say you've added a great deal of authenticity to what I do. I've always had people I've consulted with through the years. Law enforcement officers, ME's and such, but solving a case is way different."

"Glad to be of service. You ready to search?"

I nodded.

The apartment was one room. There was a twin bed in a corner, a small kitchenette with a round wooden table and a bathroom off the main room. There was a dresser in the other corner. It was plain, but serviceable and tidy.

"Why don't you start there." He pointed to the dresser. "Use these if you find something." He handed me several of the evidence bags he held in his hand.

We went to work. It felt strange going through Mr. Flynn's things. One could learn a great deal about another human by perusing their personal items. He was quite traditional in his clothing choices. Even though he sometimes fixed and sold jewelry, along with the clocks, he didn't seem to have any. Most of the dresser was filled with clothing, though I did find an old photo album. I set it aside.

After finishing with the dresser, I headed over to the bed. I'd seen some boxes underneath.

Kieran had gone through the bathroom and had moved on to the kitchen.

I sat on the floor and pulled the boxes out.

The first one appeared to be different sorts of parts for

clocks and possibly watches. The pieces were meticulously separated into smaller boxes. I shoved it back under the bed.

The next box was quite different. There were letters. All kinds of letters with different writing. Some appeared to be thank-you notes from clients. There were a couple from Mrs. Flynn when she'd been alive. They were quite sweet and basically talked about what a lovely husband he'd been. I only read the first one. I started to set those aside when I noticed one of the postmarks. It was much more recent, within the last year.

What in the world? My breath caught in my chest. How could she write to him if she was dead?

I opened the letter. The former Mrs. Flynn appeared to be very much alive. She wanted to come home and make amends with her children. She understood that she'd been terribly selfish and prayed he would allow her to return.

The letters were sad, and she sounded desperate. But she had abandoned her children, and Mr. Flynn didn't seem to want to forgive her.

I was certain his children believed she was dead. Belinda had told her so. She felt like an orphan. But did she have a mother out in the world? Even if Mrs. Flynn wasn't the greatest, why would Mr. Flynn say she was dead?

To protect his children. But they were adults now. My mind whirred with possibilities.

"Kieran, I think Mrs. Flynn might still be alive," I said.

He turned to me. "What do you mean? Declan told me years ago she died when he was a wee one. Right after his sister was born."

"I think that is what their father told them, but I have a recent letter that says she wanted to come home. It's postmarked within the last year."

"Interesting. Put them in an evidence bag. I'll have the team check out that story."

There were a few letters with nothing on the outside of the

envelope, as if they had been hand-delivered. There were five envelopes wrapped in a rubber band. The first was just a typed letter with one sentence.

You deserve to die. There was nothing to indicate who the letter had come from or what exactly they were upset about.

I opened the next one and it was the same sort of thing. It said: *You have been warned.*

"Kieran, I may have found something," I said. "These letters are all warnings and quite dire."

He knelt beside me. "Let me see." As he read through them his frown became deeper. "I'll send these to see if we can get some DNA off them."

That would take days, which probably frustrated him as much as it did me.

"At the very least, it appears there was someone threatening him, and possibly the family. The letters aren't faded like the others, so probably newer. In fact, the paper is so crisp, I'd say they'd been sent in the last year."

He glanced up at me.

"I learned a lot about aging paper and paintings for one of my books."

He grinned. "Strange, though."

"I agree. Why wouldn't they come to you? I mean, if someone really was threatening him, and it looks like that was the truth, why not go to the police?"

"Many reasons, but the most common is it had to do with something that broke the law."

I scrunched up my face.

"What?" he asked. Then he stood up and helped me to do the same. I handed him the stack of letters while I opened an evidence bag.

"Mr. Flynn just doesn't seem the type, right? He has always been kind and funny. And he quite obviously loved his family."

"You know as well as I do that people aren't always what they seem."

"That fact never fails to disappoint me."

"I've been doing this for more than half my life, and I feel the same way," he grumbled. "I've known the Flynns since I was a wee one. Mr. Flynn helped me fix my bike chain once when I'd been riding up and down Main Street. He didn't just fix it, though. He took the time to show me how to do it myself. I never forgot that. So, it's difficult for me to believe someone like that could have done something so wrong he would be threatened for it."

"Maybe he didn't do anything wrong," I said.

He cocked his head.

"Stay with me. The letters don't say he did anything wrong. Maybe it's the Donnels and the property problems. I find it strange that it doesn't point out the crime the Flynns' committed, which makes me think the sender was offended in some way. Perhaps, Mr. Flynn senior hadn't done anything he would think was wrong. That sounds very confusing but are you following me?"

"The other person took offense, but Flynn thought it was no big deal."

"Yes, exactly. I wish they were handwritten. It would be much easier to know if they came from a man or a woman."

"You're also a handwriting analyst?" He sounded surprised.

"I'm not an expert. But again, thanks to one of my books, I might know a bit more than most people. Usually, it's enough to know at least if a man or a woman wrote it, and which hand. Slants on letters are very telling."

"I'll remember that next time we have a handwritten letter we need looked at."

I laughed. "Like I said, I'm not an expert. But I learn a lot writing these mysteries."

"I don't suppose you know if this was off a printer or a typewriter?"

"That I can tell you. It was definitely a printer. The ink is too sharp to be a typewriter and the wrong sort of font."

He grinned. "You are helpful."

"Your people may also be able to track it down by the paper used. It's thicker card stock than regular printer paper. Remember, when we were searching for the paper my grandfather had used for his notes to us? And then we received some letters on the same stock?"

"I'm not about to forget that," he said.

"It's the same sort of thing. It's a special paper, probably used for invitations or something. It's a little bit less than card stock, so it might be easier to find than regular paper."

"I'll make a note of that."

"It might also lead you to wonder what type of person would use that kind of paper. Someone who owns a stationery store? Or someone who prints things out for brochures and such."

His eyebrows went up.

"You're thinking of someone," I said.

"I think you know. If you've bought anything there," he said.

My eyes went wide. "Mr. Simmons's jewelry store. His receipts are printed on this paper. I remember thinking it reminded me of staying in a nice hotel. He folded the paper and put it in an envelope. We can compare these to the one I received the other day when I bought my sister's present."

"Or we could just confront him," he said. "See what he has to say about this." He held up the evidence bag.

"I don't suppose I could come along? I mean, it's official police business."

"This is all police business," he said. "I'm having you help me gather evidence. Thanks to your new consulting status, it's not a big deal. But you still shouldn't investigate on your own."

"Right. Do you want to head over now?" I asked.

"I need to drop the rest of this at the station. And the Donnels know we are coming. I told them to all be at home when I came by at eleven."

"And they listened?"

"There might have been a wee threat that I would haul them all in if they weren't."

"Do you think that will work?"

He shrugged. "As we've said before, they aren't the brightest bunch. But none of them likes being locked up."

"Aren't they more likely to take the fifth, or whatever it is they do here, when they want to say no comment."

"They usually say no comment but wait until you meet them. Everything is a competition. I'll have a better chance if they are all together. I am worried about putting you in their crosshairs, as you like to say. I'd rather you stayed in the car, but I know how that will go."

"Or we could divide and conquer. Maybe I could talk to some of them separately."

"No. You stay by my side. And, for the record, the only reason you're coming with me is because you would try to do it on your own. I don't trust the lot of them."

I held up my hands in surrender. "Okay. I'll do what you ask."

He grunted.

"What? I will."

"We'll see."

A half-hour later we were headed out of Shamrock Cove. He turned onto a bumpy dirt road and stopped at a gate.

"Do you want me to open it?" I asked.

He'd told me to wear my wellies, as it had been raining off-and-on for days.

"I have it." He jumped out before I put my hand on the door handle.

Once he had it open, we drove through. Then he stopped and jumped out to close it again.

The road was a winding one and had several ruts. My bum hurt by the time we pulled up in front of a farm cottage which was surrounded by several barns. The stone house had a rusted tin roof. I hadn't seen many of those in Ireland. The weathered barns were in varying shades of gray. There were sheep and a few cows in pens. And several dogs running around, though, when I opened the door, they greeted me kindly.

I gave the furry beings quick pats on the head, and then there was a shrill whistle. The dogs ran to a man on the front porch of the house. He appeared to be the same age as the elder Mr. Flynn, very thin, and wore a leather vest over a black shirt and pants. The dogs sat in front of him their tails wagging.

"Detective Inspector," the man said.

"Seamus," Kieran replied. "Is the family here?"

He nodded. "All accounted for, as you requested. Though I ask that you move this along quickly as there's work to be done."

"Understood. If you answer my questions, we'll be gone in no time."

The other man shrugged. "We'll do what we can. Do I need to call a solicitor?"

"I don't know." Kieran was cagey sounding. "Do you?"

"You best come in." Seamus frowned.

We climbed up the porch and followed the man inside. Their snug was just off the entry. A fire had been lit at the far end of the room. The place was clean, the furniture probably from the eighties, but everything was very neat. These were people who took pride in their home, and I appreciated that.

Also, in a world where most people wanted whatever was the latest, or newest, furnishings, I thought it was a great idea to reuse and keep older things. We'd been lucky that our grandfather had a traditional and timeless taste when it came to furnishings. We'd both decided grandfather's place had been furnished perfectly. And we liked that his things surrounded us. Especially his books in the library, which was my favorite room in the house.

"Who is this?" Seamus asked and then pointed to me.

"She's the fancy author who moved to town," a woman said. "Her sister owns the bookstore. I like your sister," she said. "And your books aren't bad."

Kieran stiffened beside me, but I put a hand on his shoulder.

"What are you doing here? Research?" she asked.

"Yes," I lied. "The detective inspector has been kind enough to let me tag along, I hope you don't mind. Are you the matriarch of this beautiful family?"

"What does that mean? Did she just insult Ma?" One of the younger men seated on the sofa said. I bit my lip to keep from smiling.

"It means head of the family, you daft bugger," Seamus said. "You could do with reading a book yourself. This is my lovely wife, Maria. These idiots are my sons, Arnold and Sean."

"They're young," Maria defended her children. "But your father is right, reading a book wouldn't hurt."

The two on the couch glanced at one another and laughed.

Okay, not a home full of readers.

"Why is it you're here, Detective Inspector?" Maria asked.

"You know about the business with the Flynns?"

Every one of the Donnels stared at the floor, except Maria. She lifted her chin. "You know we do. But we've nothing to do with that mess. And God bless the young Declan. No parent should have to suffer the death of a child." She made the sign of the cross and she appeared quite sincere.

"My team asked you all for alibis for the days of the crimes.

We have some mixed messages, and I wanted to see if we could straighten that out."

"Oh?" She acted surprised, then she stared at her husband, who wasn't looking back.

"Seamus, Arnold, and Sean said they were at the Crown and Clover for quiz night. But Seamus had left early." He pulled out a photo from a file folder. "This is a CCTV photo time-stamped at just a few minutes before Mr. Flynn senior was attacked."

I hadn't known about that, but I kept my mouth shut.

"Care to explain?" Kieran asked.

Seamus lifted his head. "Don't know what you mean. Wasn't me. And I don't own a watch. Had no idea when I left. I only come to quiz night for the same reason as my sons, half-priced pints. Not like this lot is ever going to win."

"It's a coincidence then, that you left the pub at the same time as the attack." Kieran's voice wasn't accusatory.

"Why would I? I'm not a thief. That title belongs to Flynn and his son. Those two stole our land from my pa. Cheated at cards, he did. My da had to sign over half his inheritance. That land has been in our family for centuries."

Wow. That was quite a bit more information than I'd been expecting.

"We can put you near the clock store at the time of the attack, and you have motive," Kieran said. Still, he didn't sound accusatory. More like he stated facts and allowed the Donnels to dig a hole for themselves.

The boys jumped up. "He was with us," they said jointly.

It was all I could do not to roll my eyes as their lie was obvious.

Seamus held up a hand. "I wasn't."

"We will tell the truth in this house," Maria said firmly. "Do you understand me? Now, sit down." Her voice had a hard edge.

The boys bowed their heads and sat. "Yes, ma'am."

"I'd like to apologize for my children. They are only trying to protect their father."

It was easy to see who had the real power in this house. "I can tell you my husband was home not long after he left the pub. He texted me on the way. We had to call the vet, as one of our cows had a problem. He came straight away."

"Okay, good to know," Kieran said. "I'll need the vet's name. And to know about your sons' whereabouts. They left the pub fifteen minutes later, which falls into our time of attack."

"Texted them, didn't I?" Seamus said. "They needed to come home and help with Bess."

"Bess?"

"I think that's the cow," I whispered.

"It is," Seamus said. "Took all of us to roll her over."

"Is she okay?" I'd seen the fluffy cows when we'd pulled up. I always thought of the fuzzy Highland cows being from Scotland, but Ireland had their own version.

They all looked at me like I had two heads, including Kieran.

I shrugged. "I like your cows. They are cute," I said.

Maria smiled. "She's right as rain now. So, hopefully that settles your mind, Detective Inspector. My family was here with me helping with the livestock. The vet will back what we have said."

"Right. And when Declan Flynn was attacked? What about then?"

The sons looked at each other. That was suspicious.

"When was that?" Maria asked. "Since you seem to be so fond of timing."

Because of the rain, Kieran didn't have an exact time of death. The body had cooled more quickly, and the ME couldn't be too specific. There was almost a twelve-hour period when it could have happened. But he'd had a blow to the back of the head, so unlike the elder Mr. Flynn, he'd definitely been attacked.

Kieran gave them a time period. Though he shortened it to six hours. The mother opened her mouth, but Kieran held up a hand. "I'd like to ask your sons in private. They are adults, unless you want me to take them down to the station." He pulled out his handcuffs.

"No need for that." Maria waved her hand. "It's raining again. Feel free to use the kitchen." She pointed toward the back of the house.

"You stay here," he said to me. Then he leaned in close to my ear. "I don't want them getting their stories straight."

I nodded.

"Arnold, you first," Kieran said.

"Why me?" the young man whined.

"Do what he says," Maria said sharply.

The kid ducked his head and followed Kieran.

"It must be a full-time job keeping a farm like this going," I said. "I don't know how you do it with just the four of you."

Seamus shuffled his feet.

"When it's all you know, you don't think of it that way," Maria said. "This is our life. We do what we must to keep it going."

I nodded. "Before she took over the bookstore, my sister had a lavender farm in Texas. It was a lot of work. Still is." It occurred to me that while she'd left the place in capable hands, I had no idea if she received daily updates. I needed to ask her about that. As sweet and kind as she was, in many ways she was more of a control freak than I was. I couldn't see her letting it go. Especially since she'd worked so hard to turn the farm into a successful business.

"She mentioned that the last time I was in there," Maria said.

"Do you belong to one of the book clubs?" I was trying to

keep the topics on things that wouldn't put her on the spot. My version of good cop. But it was also a great way to get to know someone.

"I'll be a part of Lolly's next time they meet. I RSVP'd to the invitation just yesterday." She seemed quite proud of the fact.

"That should be a lively group," I said. "I've met some of her friends. And my sister and I adore Lolly. She's one of the best neighbors we've ever had."

"I can see that," Maria said. She leaned back in her chair. "She's always been kind to me."

"I'm going outside," Seamus said. "If he needs me, I'll be in the barn." Without waiting for an answer, he left.

Sean stood up to follow, but Maria snapped her fingers. "Sit," she ordered.

"The men in my family were born for a life outdoors," she said. "If they can't watch the telly and stuff their gobs, they become nervous. Why don't you have a seat?"

It was the first time she had offered. I sat down in the over-stuffed chenille chair across from hers.

"What kind of books do you like to read?" I asked. Again, it seemed an innocuous choice of conversation, but told one a lot about another person.

"I'm fond of our Irish authors, and all types of fiction. Roddy Doyle's kids novels were some of my first books. Brendan Behan's short stories I discovered at university."

I was such a snob. I hadn't expected her to have gone to college. Only because I'd heard numerous people say the family wasn't the brightest. I knew better than to judge by hearsay.

"I'm embarrassed to say I haven't read them."

"I'll make you a short list to start you out." She opened a drawer in the table next to her and pulled out a spiral notebook and pen. "I keep a list of books I've read in this." She pulled out a bound journal. "Nearly to the end, I just bought another one from your sister." Her tone and defensiveness had changed. She tore a page out of the spiral and wrote on it.

She'd just finished when Arnold walked in. "Your turn," he said to his brother.

The men smirked at one another, but Sean left.

"Ma?"

"Head out and help your father in the barn. I'll send Sean if we need you again. Just don't go too far."

"Yes, Ma."

She leaned forward and handed me a list with several names and titles. "Like I said, those will be a good start."

"What did you study at university?" I asked.

"Maths," she said. "It's how I'm able to keep this going. Was a mess when I took over."

"I suck at math," I said. "That's more my sister's thing. She always said she got the math gene, and I picked up the literary one."

She smiled and nodded. "Twins, right?"

"We are."

"I can't imagine what your mother went through. Mine are two years apart and that was close enough. Seamus may not seem like it, but he's a good father in many ways. The boys have picked up some of his habits of too much drink, mind you. And a refusal to go to church. They also like a game of darts. But they aren't bad boys."

I'd heard something quite different. Maybe this was a case of a mother's love.

"Can I ask about this feud? Was it really over a card game?"

She rolled her eyes. "Who knows? Our Irishmen like to share a story that makes them look better than they might be. My father-in-law was no different. I can tell you the transfer of property was properly done. As far as I've been able to tell, my father-in-law needed the money from the sale of the land. It had nothing to do with a game, and everything to do with staying afloat. My husband just believed his da and won't hear the truth."

"I see."

Her eyes narrowed onto me. "Do you? What happened was that when we were back in the game, my husband wanted to buy that land back. The Flynns refused. And then turned that land into one of those God-awful glamping sites. My family believes the land is meant for the animals, not for humans to pretend to be out of doors while living in fancy tents."

Her dislike for the glamping site was quite clear.

"Last I heard, they were going to build even more caravan sites, which would have possibly blocked our view on the hill out to the sea. Seamus was furious." She held up her hands. "But certainly not angry enough to kill anyone. You have to understand. This is something that has been going back and forth between the families for years. It isn't like they came to blows."

But could she be certain of that though? While she'd tried to make her sons sound harmless, they had rap sheets. Many of their crimes included assault charges for fights in pubs. Kieran had shared that information with me. The same was true for Seamus. They were all hotheads, who thought with their fists, not their brains.

"I know you may be on the outs with the family, but I'm worried about Belinda. She's been through so much. While I haven't known her long, she seems quite kind."

"Ah. Yes. She's a bright girl. Reminds me of myself in many ways. Properly educated and a step ahead of her brother, to be sure. Has a brain on her. I can't imagine how her heart must be hurting. Bad blood or not, I wouldn't wish her situation on anyone."

I nodded.

"Any idea when they will be doing a wake for young Declan?"

I wondered if she and her family thought about going.

"I imagine they are waiting for the body to be released by the medical examiner."

"I thought he was bashed on the head. What more do they need to know?"

I shrugged. "My dog found him and it was... awful. I'm sure they are trying to make every effort to find out exactly what happened. Hence, the reason Kieran came out. I know you all didn't see eye to eye, but do you know of anyone who might have wanted to hurt the Flynns?"

"I can't help you there. Though, he did like a game of cards and chess. At least, that's what I've heard. Could be he owed the wrong people some money."

"What, like organized crime?"

She laughed. "In Shamrock Cove? No. That's funny. But people around here take their games of chance seriously. You heard what my husband said. I've not paid much attention to the Flynn family the last year or so. We keep ourselves busy with the farm. It's why I joined the book club. I need an excuse to get away for a bit and have real conversations."

But what Seamus had said wasn't true. She'd made that clear when she said the land had been sold to the Flynns years ago. I didn't understand why the men thought the Flynns stole the land when they had to know the truth.

Then I remembered something my mother said long ago. If someone tells a lie often enough, it becomes truth to them. That had been regarding some bullies in high school, ones who liked to pick on literary types like me. They thought they were better than everyone else. Funnily enough, it had been my clever sister who put them in their place. She'd been a popular cheerleader. When she found out what had happened, she cornered the girls, and said I had more brains than all of them put together. Also, that she would make their lives miserable if they even looked at me again.

That was my sister. Kindest person in the world, unless you messed with someone she loved.

This was one of the many reasons I was so protective of her now.

"Do you know anything about Belinda's mother? I've been told that she passed away years ago."

She blinked and the surprise was evident. "Is that what Flynn told his children? That she was dead?"

I nodded.

"Interesting." She frowned.

"Do you know something different from that?"

"She left him when the children were young. Won herself some bit part on a television show in London. Never came back."

"So, he lied to his kids about their mother."

She shrugged. "No matter what's gone on between his family and ours, Flynn was a good father. I'm sure he did what he thought best to protect them."

Kieran came out of the kitchen, sans Sean.

"You ready?" he asked.

"Thank you for making me feel welcome," I said. "I hope you enjoy the book club." It never hurt to leave on good terms.

"I'll be seeing you," she said.

I couldn't wait to get into the car and tell Kieran everything.

After opening the car door for me, he went around to the other side.

He turned to me and laughed.

"What?"

"You're nearly bursting with news. It's all over your face," he said. "You aren't much of a poker player."

"Wrong. I'm a great poker player. But you're right, I am excited. I have so much to tell you. I found out so many things."

"Tell me everything," he said.

EIGHTEEN

By the time we made it to the cattle guard and gate leaving the Donnels' property, I'd told Kieran everything about them selling the land to the Flynns. He jumped out to open the gate. After we drove through, he closed it again.

"None of that surprises me," he said. "I'll have my team check the property records. You've come up with some good leads today. The missing wife, the threatening letters, and property status. I might keep you around."

We laughed.

"You don't think Belinda's mother is involved, do you? If she's wanting to come home, maybe she needs money. She might have broken into the store and stolen the items. The father walked in and had a heart attack when he saw her."

"So, she's gone from actress to jewel thief and possible murderer?" he asked. "And she killed her own son because he found her stash on the boat?"

"I can't imagine that last one. But people do all kinds of horrible things for money. You want pesky evidence, don't you?"

"You're learning."

"So, tell me what you found out from the brothers?"

"While I'll need to check their stories with the vet, I believe them about their alibi for the store. I can't say the same for the day of Declan's murder. I wish the ME could be more specific about time of death and that the cameras had been operable on the path behind the court."

"Do you think he was taking the path down to his boat?"

"Perhaps. It would be an easy way to stay out of view of anyone in town. While it's a well-worn path, not many take it that far down the hill. But why would they attack right behind the court where someone might find him? It would have made sense when he was further along where there is tree coverage separating the path from town."

"That is weird. It's almost like they wanted us to find him." I frowned. "Or, maybe they hadn't meant to kill him. Could be they were only trying to get his attention, but things got out of hand."

"He didn't have any defensive wounds. They caught him by surprise," he said.

"Was it premeditated?"

"No way to know until we figure out exactly what happened. It would help if the killer came in to confess."

I smiled. "I bet it would. Do they know what caused the injuries?"

"Something wooden. Possibly a cricket bat or rolling pin. The circumference is odd, according to the ME. She couldn't exactly give me specifics, though they are still testing."

"Any idea on when they might release his body for a wake?"

"That I can't say. The main autopsy has been done. They are waiting on testing and DNA results. It could be a few more days. I'll have the letters we found tested as well. I mean, you found." He grinned.

"Happy to help. Is it just me or does it feel like we're kind of back to square one?"

"I wouldn't say that. We've eliminated some of our suspects. It will give us a chance to narrow in on some others."

"Like Mr. Simmons?"

He nodded. "That paper is telling. I'd like to see him explain that one. But I want to see if we can get trace DNA off the paper first. Again, it will be a minimum of twenty-four hours. Probably closer to seventy-two."

"I know I said this before, but I keep wondering if we don't have two different assailants."

He shrugged. "We'll follow the evidence. You have great instincts, and you might be right. It could be kids broke into the store, and the surprise of it caused Mr. Flynn to have a heart attack. It's looking more like he hit the edge of the glass case on his way down. So, that could have been accidental. But someone murdered Declan. Maybe for the jewelry."

"But if it was kids who broke in, why would Declan still have the jewelry?"

"Can't say. At least, not yet. Unless he paid them to do it. As much as I hate to admit it, that's a possibility. But we've had this conversation before."

"It doesn't hurt to go back over things as we find out more information. I have a lot to write down in my notebook. I can't trust my memory anymore. Also, when I write things down, for some reason, it becomes clearer in my mind."

"I do the same thing," he said. "Where do you want me to let you off?"

"I'd like to go home, but I should check and see if Mr. Poe needs a walk. Lizzie has been very busy with the store."

"I'll drop you off there."

As he pulled up in front of the bookstore, he put his hand on my arm.

"Once you get your facts down, please don't go off investigating on your own. I've allowed you to join me to keep you out of trouble."

The allowed phrasing hit a nerve, but I bit my tongue. He was right. No other officer would let me hang out on an investigation. He'd been more than generous including me. But I had so many more questions. While he waited for DNA, I very much wanted to speak with Jessie and her father.

If her dad had found out about the romance, he could have killed Declan Flynn. That made more sense than his mother killing him. Though, weirder things had happened. And she *had* abandoned her family.

While I'd never really wanted children, I couldn't imagine leaving them behind to pursue a career. I tried not to be too judgmental about that sort of thing. Maybe if I had found a person to share my life with, I might have had kids. But I believed women had the right to pursue their dreams, whatever those might be.

It felt selfish. If she were a narcissist, she most likely justified what was in her best interest.

Kieran opened the car door, and then the door to the bookshop for me.

"Thanks," I said and waved him off.

Inside, Lizzie was busy at the front counter. I walked around.

"Do you need me to take Mr. Poe home with me?"

"Oh, that would be lovely. He's missed his lunch and his walk. Do you mind?"

"Not at all."

She called out to Caro, who was helping a customer on the first floor. "Can you watch Mercy walk home?"

I laughed. "That isn't necessary."

"It is. Kieran said so. And we're doing what he said."

Everyone looked at us with surprise. Great, now it would be all over Shamrock Cove, probably before I made it home. This town did not keep secrets.

Caro whispered something to the client, who smiled. "Come on, you," she said to me.

I hooked up Mr. Poe's leash. He was more than happy to see me when he noticed I was taking him somewhere. He adored my sister and was her protector. But all bets were off if he thought he might get some food or a treat.

We walked out the back door, and Caro watched as I made my way to the secret entrance.

For once we made it home without any sort of incident. Rob was out in his garden working and waved us over. "I heard the good detective is allowing you to go on interviews. That's new."

I grinned. "It's his way of trying to keep me out of trouble," I said. "He figures if he allows me to listen in, I won't go off on my own. Not that I ever do that on purpose."

"Right." He laughed hard.

"Mean," I said. "But true."

"I'm feeling left out. Any chance you need to do some brainstorming? I could bring over some lunch." He waggled his eyebrows. "Have you tried our Irish barmbrack yet?"

"I have no idea what that is."

"A bread we usually have around certain holidays. But I've been tweaking my recipe. I know how much you love some bread. And I have a new Irish stew. Matt at the pub won't give me their recipe, but I think I'm close."

Matt and his mom made some of the best food I'd ever had in any sort of restaurant. I didn't blame them for guarding their recipes. Rob was an amazing chef with a palate that could pick out most any ingredient.

"I'm happy to try and compare."

"Excellent. Give me a few minutes to wash up, and I'll be over."

I let myself in and then let Mr. Poe out the back door. He did his zoomies around the yard. And then sat and stared at the fairy garden near one of the trees. My sister swore he could see the wee folk, as they called fairies here. I was highly suspicious and thought there might be a squirrel or a rabbit hiding in the flora my sister nurtured. Her thumbs were as green as mine were black.

The only job I was allowed in the garden was watering and only under her careful supervision. Though, with all the rain, I seldom did even that. Rob came to the back gate and let himself in. I rushed to take one of the dishes he'd balanced precariously on his arms.

"This looks more like a feast for hundreds than an afternoon lunch."

He grinned. "Trying out some other recipes for my book. You've got a great palate, if you don't mind."

"I was just thinking about how good yours was as well. You're so good at picking out ingredients. I love that you trust me with this."

"If you ever tell him, I'll deny it, but my lovely spouse loves everything I make. I can't trust him to be honest with me."

"To his credit, I don't think I've disliked anything you've made. Well, there was that time when you pushed my heat limits with ghost peppers, but it was still tasty. Do you want to eat out here? I can get the cushions from storage." I pointed to the wooden picnic table in the garden.

"That would be grand. It's such a lovely day. I'll set up the dishes."

Mr. Poe had left the fairies behind at the first sniff of food. I brought out the plastic seat cushions Lizzie had made and put them down. She loved sitting out here, but the hard wood was tough on her bones. At least, that is what she said.

I also brought out Mr. Poe's dishes with some kibble and water.

We ate in silence, except when he served me something new.

I wasn't much of a judge, as I too loved everything he made.

But he was darn close with the stew. We didn't discuss the case, only the food. This would be his first fête with the food truck and he was understandably nervous.

When we were done, I gave him a rundown of everything that happened. I trusted our neighbors, as they had become our closest friends. They were also quite helpful in solving mysteries. I hadn't meant to leave them out, I'd just been working more with Kieran this time.

After lunch, Rob suggested a walk down the back path to see how far it was from our house to the docks where Declan's boat was. I was curious about timing, and we had no way of knowing which way he'd been headed.

What I should have been doing was writing, but I needed to walk off the carbs, and Mr. Poe had been running around the garden, but he'd settle better if I wore him out with a long walk.

We talked for a bit, as we headed to the boat slips. "So, your suspects are the grouch jeweler or his daughter. And then the Donnels? Or the mother of poor Declan, who might have come back into the picture."

"Right. Except no one has seen the latter. If she's behind this, she's hiding out well. Kieran wants to chat with the jeweler, but I think he's going to clam up the second the police show up."

"I could go with you," he said. "You've met me, I'm always up for a new watch. I promised myself I'd buy one when I finished this new cookbook."

We had that in common. Buying some sort of gift for ourselves when we finished a project. Whatever worked to make those writing goals was what I'd always thought.

The path behind the court was fairly even, but as we made our way behind the town, it wasn't as smooth. Rob crooked his arm, and put my hand through it, to keep us both upright. Meanwhile, Mr. Poe sniffed his way down. We didn't usually go this way to the shoreline. I preferred heading down Main

Street, which was well paved and an easier walk. It was also well lit, and there were witnesses. While this was a public path, not many people used it.

That was one of the reasons no one had found poor Declan's body for so long. When it was rainy and muddy, no one used this one.

"If you were hurrying, how fast do you think it would take to get from the shore to my house? Declan was tall so his stride would have been longer."

"Maybe five minutes," he said. "Since there is public parking up at the castle, which is seldom checked, he might have parked his lorry there. And then taken the back way down to his boat. People park up there all the time because we know it can be difficult in town."

That was true. The church on the hill and the castle just beyond it had the most parking. It was only a quarter of a mile or so into town.

I nodded. "Could be."

We passed a few blocks away from the pub and then came to a steep hill. We helped each other down.

"I can't imagine going up it in the rain," I said. "And it was raining fairly solid that day."

By the time we made it down to where the boats were docked, I was exhausted. That is until I saw something that made me draw in a breath.

"I can't believe it," I said.

NINETEEN

We stood by the gate to the docks, which was manned by the guard I'd met the other day. Since I had no real excuse to be there, we waited just outside his booth.

"What is it you saw?" Rob whispered.

"Jessie was on Declan's boat. What if she was looking for the jewelry?" Had she been in on the heist? Well, insurance scam. Heist seemed a bit too professional for what had happened. "She said they'd been leaving town." Had Declan told her everything? I needed to talk to her.

Mr. Poe gave up and laid down at our feet while we waited.

"What if she's staying there?" he said. "You said she and her father had been having words."

"Let's wait just a few minutes longer," I said.

The wait paid off. Five minutes later, she walked down the dock to the entrance.

I stepped out and she jumped. "Sorry, I didn't see you there." She smiled but it didn't reach her eyes. She held a tote bag. The boat had already gone through an investigation. I wondered what she'd taken off there.

"I noticed you were on Declan's boat," I said. "As you know,

I've been helping the police with their inquiries, I was curious if you found anything."

She pursed her lips, and then her face screwed up. Tears fell and she sobbed. Rob and I stared at one another. *Now, I've done it.*

"Come on, luv," Rob said. "There are some tables over here. Let's sit down." The tables were for family picnics and looked out over the marina. She followed us and sat down.

"Take your time," I said. I pulled out the packet of tissues I kept in my pocket. She took the whole thing.

"I'm sorry. It's just..." She sobbed again.

Rob patted her back. "It's okay, luv. We're here for you. Tell us how we can help."

She blew her nose. "I love your food truck," she said to Rob. "I wish you had it every day."

"Thank you for that. Tell us what is troubling you. Is it losing your Declan?" Rob was a lot like my sister. He could be kind and snoopy at the same time. It was a gift. "I've heard all about it. Is your father giving you a hard time?"

She caved in on herself. "Da isn't speaking to me. I wish I could be more upset about that, but in a way it's the best thing. I couldn't take his arguing on top of everything that happened. And people are saying Declan committed a crime. I mean, he owned the store. He could do what he wanted."

"But his father nearly died," I said.

"Right, but that was nothing to do with Declan. He took the items to sell. Yes, it was wrong, but he was trying to fund a new life for us. It was his property."

I started to argue, but Rob held up a hand. My mom's watch had been in those stolen items. They were not Declan's things. That part of all of this made me angry. He'd known exactly what he'd been doing.

"Jessie, do you know who might have wanted to hurt him? I

know you've been asked more than once. But you've had some time to think on it." Rob's voice was soft and coaxing.

"I don't. Everyone thinks it was my da. I understand why, but he couldn't do something like this. He blows a lot of hot air, but he couldn't hurt a fly."

Was that true?

"Do you know anything about your dad writing threatening letters to the Flynns?" I asked.

Her head popped up. "What? No. He wouldn't do that. Sure, they fought if they ran across one another, but that was as far as it went."

I realized I'd blurted that out. I'd be in trouble with Kieran, especially if she told her dad.

"Where did you hear that rumor?" she asked.

I cleared my throat. It wasn't a rumor. We had proof, but I couldn't risk her saying something to her father.

"There are all kinds of rumors flying around town. You know how people are," I said softly.

"It makes it all so much harder," she said. "I don't feel like I can grieve the man who I loved with everything that I am. People will judge me because they know how my da felt."

"You don't need to worry about that with us," Rob said. "We are on your side."

"He's right," I added. "Tell us how we can help."

"I want to visit the hospital, but I didn't want to upset his family. I heard his da is doing poorly, and if I could help Belinda... I feel like I should be doing something for her. She lost her brother and with her da... I loved Declan so. I feel we had that in common."

"I can ask if she would mind," I said.

Her face brightened. "Would you?"

"Of course. I can't promise what she'll say. But I will ask."

"Thank you." She blew her nose again.

"I won't tell Kieran, but can you explain why you were on the boat?" I pointed to the bag.

"I'd left a few things on there. Just some clothes and a blanket I'd made for him. It still has his smell." Her voice went hoarse, and she sobbed again.

When she settled down, I leaned forward. "Is there any chance you were with Declan when he was attacked?"

She jerked back and her face crumbled even more.

"I just thought maybe you may have seen who did it and were afraid to say anything. Was it your father?"

"No!" she shouted. "For the last time, no. My da and I may have our arguments, but he wouldn't kill someone. And for the record, he wouldn't hurt poor Mr. Flynn, either. He blusters and shouts, but he doesn't really mean it."

I wasn't so certain about that. Especially, since we'd found the threatening letters on the paper he used for receipts.

"Please know I don't want to upset you. We have to ask the hard questions to get to the truth. And there is one more thing I need to ask."

"Okay." She didn't sound like she wanted to answer anything else, and I didn't blame her. It was hard to believe that her dad might be culpable in the attacks, but she had to know it was a possibility.

"Did Declan ever talk about his mom?"

She frowned. "No. Why would he? She's been dead since he was a child. He was close to his da. He wouldn't have hurt him, if that's what you're thinkin'. He rushed back as soon as he heard about his da. He just left me there."

"Why did he do that?"

She glanced down at her hands. "I'd left my da a note that I wasn't coming back. I didn't want him to worry that I'd been snatched or something. So, I told him that I was going to start a new life. I never mentioned Declan though. I didn't want to cause more trouble with the families. But when Declan came back, I just couldn't. I didn't want to deal with Da."

"But you did come back," I said.

She shrugged. "Without the money Declan had put aside, there wasn't much I could do. I only had enough for one night in a hotel. And I didn't want to go traveling without him." She sniffled again. "Now, I'm stuck here forever."

"No, now," Rob said, "you can do anything you put your mind to, but it might take some planning. If you don't want to be a jeweler like your father, I'm sure there are all sorts of things you could try."

"But I do," she said. "I'm good at the designing. I love it. Declan and I were going into business together. We would have done it. Not here, mind you. But on a nice warm island."

I tried not to think about the fact that they may have been funding that dream with the stolen items from the shop, which included my mom's watch.

"And he never said anything about his mom?"

She frowned. "No. He never mentioned her."

Hmmm. I wondered if the kids had known the truth about their mysterious mother. Or had the elder Mr. Flynn really kept up the farce she was dead all these years to protect them from her selfish actions.

We sat with her for another twenty minutes until she had calmed down. Then she followed us back up the hill. She'd parked her car at the top of Main Street, but she didn't want to risk being seen by her father.

Rob promised to walk her to the car, so we left them at our back gate. Mr. Poe and I went inside. After wiping off his muddy paws. I gave him a treat.

"You've been a very good boy today. Now, it's time to write."

I'd just sat down at my desk, when the doorbell rang.

I sighed.

I wonder who that could be?

TWENTY

Mr. Poe ran to the door, but he didn't bark, which, usually, meant we knew the person on the other side. I peeked through the window at the top of the door and found the detective inspector waving back. He held up a pastry box and I laughed.

I let him in. "You know you don't need to bring pastries to get a cup of coffee from me," I said.

"Right. But it doesn't hurt," he said.

"True. I'm a sucker for Paisley's baked goods. She's almost as good as my sister."

We laughed. Mr. Poe put a paw on Kieran's leg. He leaned down and picked him up. Mr. Poe snuggled against him. Our dog was a very good judge of character. Kieran and I may have had our differences, but there was no doubt he was a very good man and a great detective inspector.

I made us both a cortado. Even though it was late in the afternoon, if I was going to get any writing done today, I'd need the caffeine kick.

"So why the visit?" I asked. "I would have met you wherever we need to go next."

"I had a call from the guard at the front gate at the docks.

He said you were there with a few people and that one of them had been on Declan's boat."

I sighed. There really were no secrets in this town.

I told him what we'd found out.

"She didn't seem to know anything about the mother possibly being in the picture," I said. "I don't think the elder Mr. Flynn told his kids she was still alive. I don't want to worry Belinda with that news, but we need to know if the mother has made contact."

"It will have to wait," he said. "I came from the hospital on my way here. He's taken a turn. The doctors think it will take a miracle for him to make it through the night."

"Oh no. Perhaps I should go see her."

"My grandmother and her crew have a prayer circle. They won't be leaving her alone any time soon. Gran told me as much."

"Okay, good. I don't suppose you asked Lolly about the mother," I said.

"I did. Nothing nice to say. She could never understand a woman leaving her children behind. Said she was always flirting with married men at the pub, including my grandad." He smiled. "She may be older, but my gran doesn't forget anything. That was nearly forty years ago, and she is still offended."

"I don't blame her. That couldn't have been easy on Mr. Flynn though. Do you remember anything about that time?"

"Back then, I was only here in the summers. My parents didn't move back to town until about five years after. Though, even then, I lived mostly with Gran. She was going through the loss of my grandfather, and we looked after one another."

That was so sweet, but I would never say it out loud. Kieran and I butted heads, but I was the first to admit he was a great human being.

"So, do you want to go to see the jeweler?"

"I do, but he's closed up shop for today. I sent one of my team out to his house, but he wasn't there either. So, that will have to wait."

I frowned. "Then why are you here?"

He ducked his head, and he appeared nervous.

"What is it?" I was worried. I'd never seen him nervous before.

"I wanted to see if you might want to go to the fête and the dance tomorrow night." The words spilled out so fast it took a minute for me to register what he'd said.

"With you?" My throat went dry, and the butterflies were back.

He nodded tightly.

"Like a date?" I sounded incredulous. I liked him and found him very attractive. But I was fairly certain I annoyed the heck out of him.

"Casual, like," he said.

I grinned. I couldn't stop myself. "Uh. Sure. That sounds like fun." I sounded so uncertain, and I didn't mean it that way. I was pleasantly shocked.

"It's okay to say no."

"I'm just surprised," I said. "I'd like to go with you. I just thought you found me the most annoying woman on the planet."

"You have your moments," he said.

We both laughed.

"But I also have mine," he admitted. "I enjoy your company."

"That's kind of you. I feel the same way about you," I replied honestly. "But people will talk." This town loved its gossip.

He shrugged. "They will probably think we're working on the case. Well, up until the dance. I hope you'll be my date for that as well."

Oh. My. This was definitely real. Then I frowned. "There is one thing you should know."

"What's that?"

"I took lessons when I was younger, but I have two left feet and that's not a joke. I'm a terrible dancer."

He shrugged. "We'll muddle through."

"Okay. Just don't say I didn't warn your toes."

"Noted."

We sat there awkwardly for a few seconds. I sipped my coffee, and he took a bite of pastry. I had a feeling my cheeks were bright pink.

"I've been wondering something, but I didn't ask her," I said, trying to move to a new subject.

"Ask who?"

"Jessie, the girlfriend. She claimed all she wanted from the boat was a blanket and a few clothes she'd left there."

"Right."

"What if she didn't know we'd found the stolen goods?"

His eyebrows went up. "You think she was trying to find them?"

I nodded. "She seems pretty desperate to get out of Shamrock Cove, and away from her father. She left him a note that she was leaving town. And then she had to come back because she didn't have any money for her travels."

"Her da didn't mention that when I spoke to him about her."

I shrugged. "Maybe he was protecting her."

"Or himself. It would be embarrassing for his daughter to run away from him. Even if she's an adult."

"True. And I know he had an alibi for the elder Mr. Flynn, but what about Declan?"

"Says he was at the shop. We checked the CCTV, and he didn't leave."

I bit my lip.

"What?"

"He didn't leave the shop out to Main Street, but what if there is a back way? All the shops have back doors, and the CCTV on the alleys isn't up yet. Or at least, it wasn't a few days ago."

"Hmm. You make a good point."

"Wait, if you know he closed the shop early today, it means you were planning to go there. And you were going to talk to him without me."

He shrugged. "No, as I mentioned I asked one of my team to check if he was in." He cleared his throat. "Not that I have to explain why I would investigate a case." He cocked his head and grinned.

I scrunched up my face. "Right. Apologies. I'm just very curious what he has to say about those threatening letters. You don't think he skipped town, do you?"

"He has no idea that we know about them, right?"

"Right."

"We'll catch up with him. In the meantime, I wondered if you wouldn't mind helping me with something. I still have several of my team out with the flu and I'm stretched thin at the station. Plus I'm keeping a full-time guard at the hospital to watch out for the Flynns."

"You know I'm always happy to help."

He pulled out a small hard drive from his jacket pocket and then handed it to me.

"That is for your eyes only," he said. "It's CCTV from the train station for the times we think Declan and Jessie might have left and returned. I also need you to keep an eye out for his mother."

"But we don't know what she looks like," I said.

He pulled out a piece of paper with a passport photo. "She's been out of the country but came back a few weeks ago. She landed in Dublin, but then there is no trace of her. We couldn't find credit cards, hotels, anything."

"She's like a ghost," I said.

"Or using someone else's identity."

Those words sunk in. "You think she's bad news, don't you?"

He nodded.

"Because she left her children behind?"

He shrugged. "Except that she was in Spain for some time, which we only know because of her passport, and that she landed back here, there is very little about where she's been the past thirty years. She supposedly left to be an actress, and she was in London right after she left here. She went to America after that, but then we lost all trace of her.

"I even have Interpol involved, but she's a low priority for them. At the very least, I'm hoping you'll find out if and when she arrived here. If I can place her in town, she'll become our prime suspect."

"But we know Declan stole the items."

"Yes, but he wouldn't have hurt his father. I can't say the same about her. What if she broke in looking for something, thinking he would be out at the farm?"

"That makes sense."

"She might have been after some cash, and then surprised Mr. Flynn."

"Seeing his wife after all those years would have been a shock. Maybe even enough to cause a heart attack. Does that mean that our jeweler is no longer a suspect?"

"Not at all. Everyone is still on the table, but now it's time to use our facts to narrow down where everyone was at the times of the crimes. The quicker we can see where everyone was, the better. I have a few days on that hard drive of the train station. I also have a camera from the bakery, which we just found out about. The night in question is on there. I was hoping you could go through it and flag times you see anything suspicious or one of our suspects."

I grinned.

"What?"

"We've come a long way for you to trust me with this," I said.

He laughed. "I have to admit, if I weren't stretched so thin, it wouldn't be happening. But I'd be grateful for the help."

"Of course."

"Thanks."

He glanced at his watch. "I need to get back to the station to relieve Sheila. She hasn't had a chance for lunch yet. She'll be mad at me."

"Take her the rest of those pastries and she'll forgive you quickly. She's like me. She can't resist."

"True. Good idea. Text or call if you find anything."

"I will."

After he left, I turned on the fire in my office, and Mr. Poe curled up in front of it. We'd already had a long day, and he softly snored as I hooked up the hard drive to my computer. Using my preview film app, I was able to pull up the videos. There were thirty-eight hours to go through.

That was a lot. And I really needed to write, but finding a murderer or murderers was more important. I would do my part.

I glanced at the passport photo Kieran had printed out. The wife had red hair and wore a lot of makeup. Though, she did look younger than a mother of adult children.

Human behavior fascinated me. It was why I did so much research into motives before writing my novels. Lizzie and I had such a wonderful mother. I couldn't imagine her leaving us. And we knew, now, that our father never had any idea we'd been born. Our mom thought he had deserted her and never tried to reach out. We hated that she believed that until the day she died.

Our grandfather had made that clear in the many letters he'd written to us. He had hidden the secret letters all over his bookstore and in his personal library a few doors down from my office. We loved getting to know him, even though it would have been much easier if he'd left everything in one spot. Or maybe, if he'd included them with his will.

But, like me, he enjoyed games and a good mystery. He thought this would be a fun way to understand him. From his friends and people who had known him we'd discovered that he was brilliant, kind, and a good person.

We only wished we'd had an opportunity to get to meet him before he died.

I put on my reading glasses. And pushed play on the videos. I was able to skip through to just when the trains arrived and departed, which helped to save time.

I opened my notebook and waited as people disembarked. No one on the first train was one of our suspects.

I pressed fast forward to the next train. Again, nothing.

Then later that night, I saw Declan and a woman, who looked like Jessie from behind, get on the train. I wrote down the time.

Hmmm. That's odd. The timing was off. If the camera was set to the correct time, it would have meant that Declan and Jessie still would have been in town when the robbery happened.

I texted Kieran.

TWENTY-ONE

While I waited for Kieran to respond, I went through the security tapes. I was surprised to see my friends, sister and myself coming from the pub the night of the first attack. We were laughing and chatting. What I hadn't been aware of was that someone had been following us. He appeared to have gray hair, but he wore a cap and kept his head down. His hands were in gloves, only a bit of gray hair sticking out from the hat gave him away.

Or did it?

Could this be John Doe? A.K.A. our father? I had no evidence to prove he was still alive. But the man in the hospital could have been him. The problem with that line of thinking was why wouldn't he come forward? Was he upset we'd inherited our grandfather's home and business? Did he want it all back?

That made my stomach churn. We loved our life here on the court.

I had no idea why I thought it might be him. It was just a gut feeling. Again, though, why hadn't he come forward and helped care for his father toward the end? When we crossed the street to check on the clock store, the man paused for a few minutes. Then as the police arrived, he turned and went the other way.

As far as I knew, our father wasn't in trouble with law enforcement. He'd been listed as missing on a mission long ago. My grandfather believed he was dead.

But someone had been watching us since we arrived.

I made some notes of the time and date, separate from what I'd been doing for Kieran.

I clicked on another file at the train station. I watched until my eyes burned, but I didn't see any hint of Mr. Flynn's former wife. All I had found was Declan and Jessie leaving on a later train than had been previously thought. The police could talk to her about that. Their timeline was seriously skewed, but why would they risk hurting his dad? That part didn't make sense.

I went back and forth between the Main Street tapes and the train station, just so I didn't get too bored with one or the other.

I'd been so engrossed I jumped when my sister called to me from the front door.

Mr. Poe ran toward her. I glanced up as she reached my office door.

"Are you busy writing? Good for you."

I made a face.

She rolled her eyes.

We laughed.

"I'm doing some video research for Kieran. He's short-handed."

"Wow, he is really starting to trust you, bringing you in like this." She waggled her eyebrows.

"I think he's just trying to keep me from getting killed by forcing me to do desk work."

"Really? I heard he asked you to the fête and the dance."

I'm sure my eyes were the size of saucers. "How could you possibly know that? He just asked me a few hours ago."

She grinned. "Well, we didn't know specifically, but the florist said he ordered flowers to be delivered tomorrow. We were all trying to figure out who he might be dating."

"This town."

"I know, isn't it great?"

"No. I have no privacy. Sometimes I miss New York. And I've been thinking of backing out." I hadn't until she told me everyone knew about our date.

"You can't do that."

"I can. What if it goes horribly wrong? Then he won't include me on investigations."

"Good. You'll be safer."

I sighed. "I know you don't understand this intense need I have to solve things, but now that I've started, I can't stop."

She scrunched up her face. "I do get it. I'm the same way, but I don't like the danger it puts us in and sometimes it is scary when we get a little too close to the truth."

She wasn't wrong.

I held up a hand. "I have a mystery I know you'll want solved," I said. "Come look at this."

I showed her the video of the man following us the night of the attack on Mr. Flynn.

"Do you think he's the killer?" she asked and was obviously confused.

"No. He's watching us."

"Even creepier," she said.

"I think it might be our dad," I said the words softly.

She frowned. "Why would you think that?"

"The John Doe in the hospital. The fact that we quite often feel like we're being watched when we are out and about. I thought, at first, it might be my stalker from New York. But what if it is our dad?"

She shrugged. "Then why hasn't he come forward? Why skulk around in the shadows like some sort of creeper?"

"I have no idea how to answer that one. Except, he might think we want nothing to do with him. Maybe he believes we hate him for not being there for us and Mom."

"But we don't," she said. "We know from his letters to Grandad that neither of them knew about us."

"I have so many questions," I said. "If he was back, why didn't he contact Grandad before he died? That makes it seem like he wasn't a very good person."

"You know how we used to make up stories about our dad. Like he was killed in a war. Or was a spy and left to keep us safe?"

"Yes."

She shrugged. "What if that's true? Or maybe he had some mental problems and has been locked up. If it is him, he's being very cautious for some reason. Or we could just have a run-of-the-mill stalker. It wouldn't be the first time for you."

I shivered. She wasn't wrong. Someone had the nerve to go through my apartment when I'd lived in New York. At first, I thought I'd been losing my mind, but then, after viewing some security tapes in our building, the police discovered I did indeed have someone breaking into my place. That had happened about the same time my mom became ill, so I left for Texas. And I never went back.

Then we moved here.

But had that person followed me? I kept going back and forth about that.

"So, what were you looking for on the security tapes?"

"Timelines for our suspects. And to see if Declan's mother shows up on the train."

"Wait. You said that but it didn't connect in my brain. His mother? I thought Belinda said she was dead."

"That was what everyone was supposed to think. But she'd been writing letters to Mr. Flynn and doing it recently. She wanted to be a part of her children's lives again. But she had abandoned them, and I don't think Mr. Flynn wanted her around."

"I can't imagine a mother abandoning her children, though I try hard not to judge people. Perhaps she mentally couldn't handle it, which is sad. That happens."

"It appears she left for a career in acting. I did a search earlier. Except for a commercial years ago, I couldn't find anything other than a few small theater gigs that she did."

"So, she left her children and husband for a career that went bust. Now, she wants back in their lives."

"And if he said no, she might have killed him. Though I don't see her on any of the videos yet. She didn't take the train in, but that doesn't mean she didn't drive."

"It would be easier to avoid cameras at the station that way," Lizzie said. "But wouldn't they have traffic cams?"

"On the Irish country roads? I don't think so."

"Surely there is one at the stop coming into town. Maybe you should ask Kieran about that one."

"Oh. Good idea. I will."

"I have to check on our book booth in an hour or so. I was hoping you and Mr. Poe could walk down with me. Caro and some of our summer interns are setting it up."

"They've arrived?"

"They did. And it's a good crew. Two young college girls, and a boy, who may know more about books than all of us put together. Rikki, Ronda, and Justin are their names."

"Did you get them set up at the cottage?" We'd bought a summer cottage on the cliff for the interns. My sister didn't want them spending their hard-earned pay on rent, which could be pricey this time of year. I bought the home as an investment. It would be rented throughout the year by an estate agent I hired. Or at least it would be once the interns went back to school.

She laughed. "They were ecstatic over how big it was. Thank you again," she said. "You didn't have to do that. I could have used the store's profits."

I shrugged. "It's a tax write-off and according to my accountant, I can use all of those I can get."

She laughed. "So, will you go down with me? I don't want to walk at night alone."

"Of course. I've been sitting all afternoon; my legs could use a stretch."

After a quick dinner, I headed down the hill with my sister. She'd put together a box of cookies for the folks at the booth. It was just the way she was made. She was always thinking of others.

The shore, and jetty had been transformed into a fairyland, as well as the surrounding cliffs. Several temporary booths had been set up on the jetty with wares from local artists and shop owners. Everything was dressed in twinkling lights.

There were also several food stalls and Rob, our neighbor, had moved his food truck down here. Though he wasn't open yet.

On the cliffs were all types of carnival rides and games. That would all be up and running by tomorrow morning. Tonight, was for setting up the summer fête, as they called it here.

It reminded me of when we were kids and Mom took us to the Texas State Fair, though this was on a much smaller scale.

At the booth, which had been painted the same deep blue

as the interior of the bookstore, Lizzie introduced me to the interns.

"Oh. My. Gawd. I love your books," Ronda said. She had a heavy Irish brogue, and bright-pink hair.

"Me, too," Rikki added. She was blue-eyed and blonde. She had an English accent, and I wondered how she'd ended up in university in Ireland. Though they had amazing schools here. "We can't believe we're meeting you in person."

I grinned and shook their hands.

"You're quite accurate in your portrayal of the detective," Justin said. He was a serious young dude. He was black, and had cool designs etched into his haircut. But he wore round glasses that gave off a bookish vibe.

"Uh. Thanks. How do you like the cottage? Everyone settling in okay?"

"We love it," Rikki said. "It's so much better than the dorm. You have all been so kind. None of us have ever interned with someone who added accommodation. I'll be able to save money for next term."

"I'm glad you like it," I said.

"Okay, so how are we with the organizing of the books?" Lizzie asked Caro.

"Everything has been alphabetized by author and then section," Caro said. She pointed to the small signs. One said: Beach Reads. Another read: Mysteries. And so on. There were about six different choices and then she planned to have vouchers ready for those who wanted to order a favorite book, and she'd have it available at the store.

My sister was quite the businesswoman.

A few booths down, I noticed Jessie was doing some last-minute touch-ups on her father's booth. "I'll be back in a minute," I said.

I walked down to her. "Did you make up with your father?" I asked.

She jumped and dropped the paintbrush.

I picked it up for her and handed it back.

"He still isn't speaking to me, but he did leave me a note to touch-up the booth. I guess that is more than I expected from him," she said.

"It's nice of you to help out, even though you are at odds."

She shrugged. "What else am I going to do? I gave Declan all the money I saved for our wedding. And the police have no idea where it is. So, I have nowhere to go but home."

I would have felt sorry for her, but she'd lied about the timeline the night Mr. Flynn was attacked.

"Has Kieran talked to you about the statement you gave?"

She had started painting again but then turned to face me. "He left messages, but I don't feel like talking to the police. Everyone can bugger off for all I care. I need time to grieve." She gave me a look that meant, you too.

"The thing is…"

"Just spit it out," she said.

"You said you were in Dublin when Mr. Flynn was attacked. But the tape from the train station shows that you were both still here in town."

She pointed a finger at me. "He didn't hurt him," she said. "Declan loved his da. Even though we weren't telling our parents the truth, he wouldn't have hurt anyone."

"Right. But there is one thing that doesn't feel right." There were many things, but I decided to focus on one.

"Yes?"

"Declan stole the jewels and watches from the store but then left them on the boat. You never gave us a good reason as to why."

"Technically, it wasn't stealing. He owned the store. Those things belonged to him."

"Not my mom's watch." I stood with my arms crossed. "That was my property."

She jerked back. "I didn't know. I thought he just took some things to sell later. And they were on the boat because…"

"Why?"

"After we were married in Dublin, we were going to sneak back. We were going to take the boat and head to Wales. We couldn't get married here. Everyone would know in a matter of minutes if we went to the courthouse." She wasn't wrong about that. "But in Dublin… we heard about what had happened at the clock shop.

"But he didn't hurt his da. That is the truth." She was vehement about that fact. "We may not have been honest with our families, but we would never do them physical harm."

"And you were on the boat looking for the stolen items, right? You weren't really after the clothes and blankets you left there. That's what you told Rob and I."

"No comment."

"I'm not the police," I said.

"Right, but you work with them. And, like you said, the items had already been picked up by the police. I didn't know that though. I'm not sure what I would have done if I had found them. I have no idea how to sell them. But I feel quite desperate to get away from here. My da… he's making life hard.

"And as for the timing of when we went to catch the train. No one said specifically when Mr. Flynn was attacked. We were rushing to catch the second-to-last train to Dublin. I had no idea what time it was or when Declan's father was attacked. I can guarantee, my Declan had nothing to do with it."

There was something in her eyes that said she had so much more to tell. But then she turned away. "I need to get this done."

I opened my mouth to ask her something else but then closed it. I'd leave the rest of the interrogation to Kieran, and there would be one. I liked Jessie, but there was something she wasn't telling us.

Could she have hurt someone? Maybe killed her fiancé for

cancelling their plans. The thought just popped into my brain. She'd just said she was desperate. And when people felt like they had no other choice, they sometimes made horrible decisions.

That fact, the one where Declan hadn't hurt his dad, I believed. There had been so much love between them. But then who broke into the store that night? Maybe it was kids.

But I wasn't so sure about that. If only the cameras facing the store had worked. Ugh.

By the time I made it back to the book booth, they were closing and locking the wooden shutters.

We all walked down the jetty together. The college students headed up the cliff to the cottage, and Lizzie and I walked with Caro back to the bookstore. Mr. Poe was exhausted. It had been a long day for him. So we crossed through the bookstore and out the back door.

Lizzie scooped him up and carried him through the secret door and into the house.

"I have an early day tomorrow. I'm going to head on up. Come on, little dude."

She carried him up the stairs like a baby. He yawned over her shoulder. I laughed. Mr. Poe was quite the character and had helped fill a gaping hole in our lives. But what I loved most about him was the way he looked after my sister.

I thought about looking at the security tapes again, but my book was calling. Sometimes the best way to solve a crime was to walk away from it for a bit. So, I lost myself in my novel.

When I glanced at my watch, it was nearly three a.m., and I thought I heard a noise outside. I waited to see if Mr. Poe came down, but he didn't. The wind had picked up. I grabbed an umbrella from the stand and quietly unlocked the front door.

Our gate had swung open.

Ugh. Had someone been in our garden?

I glanced around, but didn't see any menacing shadows. But

I was certain we'd locked the gate tight. It didn't just open on its own. In fact, it was tricky to unlock on both sides.

I shut it again and then went back inside.

It was just the wind.

But no matter how hard I tried to convince myself that was the case, my gut told me someone had been standing in our garden.

TWENTY-TWO

I woke up the next morning to someone banging on the door. "Mercy, are you all right?" Kieran called out through the door.

"I'm coming," I said. I pulled on a hoody over my T-shirt and sweats. I glanced at myself in the mirror by the front door and then tried to smooth down my hair. It didn't do much good. "What's up?" I asked as I opened the door.

"I was worried when you didn't answer my texts this morning. Are you okay?"

"I had a late night, uh, writing," I said. I didn't want to make a big deal about the gate, but I hadn't been able to go to sleep for a long time. I'd listened for any sort of noise until I heard my sister get up with Mr. Poe.

"Oh." He stopped in the hallway. "When you didn't answer…"

"You were worried the killer had me?"

"Well, it has happened before."

I grinned. "Why were you texting?"

"I planned to stop by the jewelry store to ask about the threatening letters. And then I have Mac Bannon coming into the station around noon."

"Mac Bannon?" The name sounded familiar, but I couldn't remember.

"The property developer who wanted to buy the Flynns' store."

"Right. Sorry. My brain is mud. He was the guy who owned the black SUV that was parked outside the clock shop, wasn't he?"

"He was indeed."

"Why don't you go make yourself, and me, a coffee. Let me get a quick shower. Five minutes max."

He nodded and headed off to the kitchen.

I kept my promise and was quick to shower and dress. I put my hair up in a ponytail. I checked the weather app, which promised a sunny day. I went with jeans and a long-sleeved graphic tee. My T-shirt said: 'Writer at work' on the front. And then on the back it said: 'Thinking of Ways to Kill You'. I added new white sneakers.

Kieran was at the kitchen table eating a muffin and drinking coffee. "I helped myself," he said.

"That's why she makes them. So I will eat. She knows if I have to cook, or put the mildest effort into it, I won't."

We laughed.

"I like your shirt," he said.

"It's one of my favorites and happens to be true. I make up stories for people I see all the time."

"I do that as well, though usually it's more of what kind of crimes they would have committed."

I grinned.

While we ate two muffins each and sipped a couple of cups of coffee, I told him about my conversation with Jessie and the timeline I'd seen on the train station CCTV.

"However, I didn't see the mother." Her passport photo was burned into my brain. "I wrote everything down for you. One thing, and why I questioned Jessie on my own, was because she lied. They were still in town when Mr. Flynn was attacked."

"But they may not have known," Kieran said. "They were rushing to catch the train."

"That's what she said. I still feel like she's hiding something, but I have no idea what it is."

"Is that your gut or facts?"

I kept the eye roll to myself. "I think you know."

He laughed. "Ready to go?"

I nodded.

We walked down the back alley and crossed at the corner near the pub to the jewelry store.

There was a sale sign up saying everything was fifty percent off.

"Wow. I should have waited to get that birthday gift for my sister. I could have saved some cash."

We grinned at each other. "Maybe he'll give you the discount."

"He doesn't seem the type."

When we walked in, I was first. The owner saw me and smirked. And then he saw Kieran. He plastered a smile on his face. "Detective Inspector, how can I help you?" There was something not right about this guy, but was he a murderer?

"I have some more questions for you," Kieran said.

"Do I need my solicitor?" he said it as a joke.

"If you do, we can go straight to the station and do this more formally." Kieran didn't take his bait.

It was all I could do not to laugh at the expression on the jeweler's face.

"No. No. Ask away."

"Right. Have you ever seen these before?" He pulled up the letters on his phone. The threatening ones that had been on the paper he used for receipts in his store.

He frowned. "Of course not. Why would I?" But there was an odd tone in his voice.

"Are you certain?" Kieran asked. "I have proof it came from your printer, and this is the same grade of paper you use."

His eyes widened with surprise. "I. Uh. Do I really need my lawyer?"

"Again, that's up to you. As I said, we can question you formally at the station."

The jeweler glanced over at me. "It was years ago," he said. "It's an old fight. I hadn't sent him one of those in years."

"But you did threaten him?" Kieran said. His voice had turned deadly. It was exciting to watch him work.

"Only because back then he was encroaching on my business. They started repairing jewelry and reselling items along with their watches and clocks. My family has owned this business for more than a hundred years. So, yes. We argued. But he gave as good as he got. It wasn't all me."

"Did you hate him enough to kill him?" Kieran said the words quietly.

The jeweler held up his hands in surrender. "Now, Detective, I would never. Did we argue for most of our lives? Yes. Did I ever attack him or hurt his kids? No. And there's no way you can prove that I did."

"I wouldn't be so sure," I said the words before I realized it.

Henry Simmons went white.

Kieran gave me a look.

I shrugged. "Only that evidence is stacked against you. And even more so that when you found out about your daughter and Mr. Flynn's son, you were furious."

"I... of course I was angry. But I wouldn't have killed anyone over it. Besides, I didn't find out until poor young Declan was dead, did I? Jessie told me what happened when she came home with her tail between her legs. But I took her back in out of the goodness of my heart."

That right there was why I didn't like this guy. He was so mean to his daughter. She'd been through the wringer, and even though she was hiding something, she didn't deserve to be disrespected. People couldn't always choose who they loved. Even though I steered away from relationships, I'd seen that was the case more than a few times.

"If you have any other questions, I'm afraid we will have to do this formally," Simmons said. "I feel like you're trying to trick me into a confession."

"No tricks, only evidence," Kieran said. "But we're done for now. Don't be leaving town, Mr. Simmons."

Something flickered in the man's eyes, but he nodded.

We walked out.

"Where are we off to now?"

"Station. You can't be in the room when I speak with Bannon, but you can watch through the computer."

I laughed.

"What?"

"You really are trying to keep me from questioning the suspects on my own."

"Hasn't helped. You spoke with Jessie yesterday." He gave me the eye.

I grinned. "The opportunity presented itself. Besides, she is still hiding something. I can tell. She knows something about Declan's death or Mr. Flynn's attack. But she clammed up when I tried to push her."

"Or she could just be grieving her loved one. You understand better than most about that."

"You aren't wrong. I'm surprised Mr. Bannon isn't bringing his lawyer along."

"Oh, I'm certain he is. And I expect we'll get a load of no comments, but I must do my due diligence. He's been trying to buy up properties for the last year. I've had more than one complaint over his strong-arm tactics."

"In the fictional mysteries, it's always the husband, wife, or property developer."

He chuckled as he opened the door of the station.

"They here yet?" he asked Sheila.

"Put them in interview one."

The station was a small cottage with a couple of offices, and two interview rooms. It looked more like a storybook home with floral wallpaper than a police station. They had eight police officers who worked our town, and a smaller station in the town down the road. But since half of his team was still off with a summer flu, I was lucky enough to get to observe.

I was determined to behave myself so that, maybe, he'd let me do this sort of thing in the future.

He motioned for me to sit down at his desk. And he pulled up the camera in the interview room. He hit play and I could see the property developer and his lawyer move and speak. They whispered something and then faced straight forward.

"Probably trying to get his story straight."

As he started to walk out. I yelled out, "Wait."

He turned back. "What is it?"

"In addition to getting his whereabouts for the murder and the attack, ask him if he was talking to Declan without his father's knowledge." That thought had just come to me.

Kieran frowned.

"Stay with me here. Declan was running away with Jessie. The store was in his name. Maybe he was doing what his father wouldn't and selling the store."

Kieran nodded and made a note on his tablet.

When he walked into the interview, he just nodded. He didn't say anything. He pushed a button on the recorder. Then he opened the thick file folder he'd carried in. I'd seen that on a television show. It would make the suspect think they had a lot of evidence against him.

He didn't say anything for more than a minute. He just flipped through the papers in the folder.

"What's going on?" Bannon asked. He had a heavy Irish brogue. His hair was slicked back, and he wore a golf shirt. His face was sunburned, as if he'd been on the course recently. And his red hair was streaked with white.

His lawyer was a balding man in a dull gray suit. He put his hand on Mac's arm. I guessed to keep his client quiet.

"Thank you for your patience," Kieran said. His tone was friendly. "I was refreshing my memory. So, when my men questioned you, you stated you were in Dublin at the time of the attack on Mr. Flynn. Correct?"

Mac glanced at his lawyer, who nodded.

"Right," Mac said.

"Except, we have this. I'd like you to notice the timestamp." He pushed across a photo. I couldn't see it from my vantage point, but I was very curious.

Mac and his lawyer glanced at one another.

"Timestamps can be manipulated," the lawyer said.

"Except when they are CCTV cameras. And it isn't the only one we have." He showed them another picture.

Mac's eyes opened wide, and he sat back in his chair.

"Both of these photos show that you were in town an hour before Mr. Flynn's store was broken into." He shoved another picture forward. "And this one is for the time of young Declan's murder."

Mac opened his mouth, but his lawyer put a hand on his arm again. "No comment," the property developer said.

Kieran shook his head. "That's fine, but I have you in town at the time of both crimes. We also have several witnesses at the pub who claim you had quite the row with the elder Mr. Flynn just a few days before his attack."

We still weren't certain it was an attack. From the last I

heard, the ME said it might have been an accident. But something or someone had caused him to have a heart attack.

"Witnesses say the fight became quite aggressive with Mr. Flynn claiming he'd sell to you over his dead body."

"No comment."

Kieran grinned. "You can say that all you want, but you are on the pub cameras. I have video. You aren't helping yourself by claiming no comment."

"I didn't hurt the old geezer," he said.

"Mac," the lawyer chastised.

"I'm not going to let this bloke stitch me up. It's true. I was putting the pressure on. His son was open to selling and the old man had signed the store over to him. But he refused to even let Declan think about it."

"So, you attacked the old man, and then killed Declan, thinking the sister would sell quickly?" Bam. Kieran had thrown that down quickly.

Mac jerked back. "What? No. I told you, I wasn't there that night. And why kill Declan? With his dad on his deathbed, he would have been more willing to sell."

"Mac," his lawyer said loudly. It was like a slap.

"Shut up," Mac said. "I'm not going down for murder."

"So, we've established you were in town, and you lied about your alibi. I can get you on obstructing justice at the very least." Kieran stared at the lawyer. "Tell me where you were?"

"Rented one of those cottages on the cliff. Been seeing a… woman when I'm in town. When your team questioned me, my wife was in the office. I couldn't very well tell the truth, could I?"

"I'll need a name and address where we can speak to her."

Mac glanced at his lawyer. The lawyer nodded.

"And you won't tell my wife?"

"I make no promises," Kieran said. "These things have a habit of getting out, but it won't be from my department."

"Moira Brighton. She's an actress. And old Flynn's ex-wife."

Well, that was news.

TWENTY-THREE

After that revelation there was silence for a full minute in the interview room. No doubt the detective inspector wanted to give Mac Bannon a chance to explain himself. But the property developer sat there with his solicitor and didn't say a word.

"And when did you and Ms. Brighton meet?" Kieran asked.

I was confused by the name Brighton, though many actors picked stage names. Or, perhaps, she'd gone back to her maiden name. I'd do some research later. That wasn't the name on her passport.

"About a year ago. It was her suggestion that I should take a look at Shamrock Cove as a place for my new resort and shops."

"When did you first approach the Flynns?"

Bannon shrugged. "I don't remember the exact dates, but not long after she told me about the place."

"And how did the elder Mr. Flynn take the news at first?"

"Like you might imagine. Hostile," Bannon said. "Didn't want anything to do with me. But then I found out that, technically, the son had controlling interest of the business and owned the building. So, I'd been meeting with him secretly the last month or two."

"And when did you become aware that Ms. Brighton was the ex of Mr. Flynn?"

Bannon made a face. "I didn't know anything about that until a few weeks ago. She was afraid someone saw us in public and she was upset. I didn't understand why it would matter. I'm married and the one with everything to lose."

"Do you have any idea who that someone might have been?"

"I told her we could go back to Dublin and stay in one of my houses there. But she insisted on staying in Shamrock Cove. Said she wanted to make amends with her family. That's when I found out she had kids. I honestly had no idea she was old enough to have adult children. She's quite fit."

But had she reached out to her children? I didn't think so. I had a feeling Belinda would have brought it up. And why, if she was so concerned about her kids, hadn't she come forward to help her daughter during such a trying time?

They finished the interview, but as they were walking out I accidentally bumped into Mr. Bannon. I had a question that wouldn't wait.

"Sorry about that," I said. "But since I have you, can I ask you one more question?"

The lawyer gave him a look. Bannon started to push past me. I put a hand on his arm. "I just need to know if Ms. Brighton was with you the night of Mr. Flynn's accident. You said you had a cottage where you were staying."

"Who are you?" he asked.

"She's a consultant working on the case, but it is a good question," Kieran said.

Bannon looked at his lawyer who nodded.

"She wasn't there when I first arrived," he said. "She maybe showed up a half-hour later. Close to eight. But she had groceries and some flowers. So that's where she'd been."

They walked out of the police station.

"We need to find Moira Brighton," I said.

"I've already texted the team. We'll send out an alert."

"That last bit was very informative," I said.

"Why is that?"

"Because the grocer and the florist close before six. And it was almost two hours later when she arrived at the cottage. She was giving herself an alibi."

His eyebrows went up. "You're right."

My gut told me that Moira had surprised Mr. Flynn that night. Her sudden appearance may have triggered a heart attack. The surprise of it all. But then she just left him there to die.

And would she have attacked her son? That part didn't make sense.

We needed to find Moira.

Later that afternoon, Mr. Poe and I headed down to the book booth on the jetty. It was a beautiful sunny day, and there were tons of folks milling about. A line had formed in front of the booth and curved around the corner. Rikki, one of the interns, was walking up and down the line handing out sticky notes.

What is that all about?

I knocked on the side entrance, and my sister let me into the booth.

"What's with the line?" I whispered.

She grinned. "It's for your signing. Some of them have been waiting for hours in case we ran out of books."

"Oh. I wasn't expecting a crowd," I said. If I were honest, I hadn't really thought about it. People were here for the fair, and I didn't think they'd care about books.

"Because you never realize how popular you and your

novels are," Lizzie said. "Don't worry, though. I bought twice as many as we thought we might need. Caro is also doing online orders at the bookstore. You'll need to sign even more tomorrow so we can ship them out."

"Anything I can do to help out. Even if my hand falls off." I grinned at my sister's excitement.

"I had Rikki bring down a stool for you to sit on, and she's giving the fans a sticky note to make the personalization easier for you."

"I appreciate that." It was embarrassing when you had to ask someone like a Joe, how to spell their name. But sometimes it was with an e, sometimes without. Same with Ann. The sticky notes would help with that.

"I can give you two hours, but then..."

"What?" She frowned.

"I have a get-together."

"Do you mean your date?" She grinned.

"I don't think we're calling it that. Why would you call it that?"

Her eyebrows went up. "Oh, I don't know, Mercy. Maybe because he finds any excuse he can to come by the house. And he's involving you in the case."

"It's not like that. We just get each other and have a mutual interest in solving crimes."

She laughed even harder. "Right." She took a deep breath. "Whatever works for you."

I decided to change the subject. "Can you ask the interns to keep an eye out for this woman?" I showed her the passport photo of Moira Brighton.

"Who is that?"

I gave her a brief explanation.

"Really? Why wouldn't she contact her children or go to the hospital? Poor Belinda is handling everything on her own. That is so wrong."

"I don't disagree. From what I can tell, and it's only from the outside looking in, I'm certain we're dealing with a big-time narcissist."

"She'd have to be to leave her children like that."

"Agreed."

"It's time for the signing," Ronda said from the other side of the booth. "I brought you down a cushion, Ms. McCarthy. It looks like you may be sitting for some time."

"Thanks. And please call me Mercy. Ms. McCarthy was our mom."

The young woman blushed.

While my sister sold books to people who passed by, Ronda and Rikki kept the line flowing while I signed books for the readers. As usual, the time went by quickly. My hand was cramping as I signed the last book they had available. There were a few people left in the line.

Lizzie went over to them. She handed them cards. "This is our email. We'd be happy to send you a personalized copy at the end of the week when our new shipment comes in. Just fill out the information and take it to the register. We'll get you set up."

I felt bad that they had waited so long, but when I glanced past them, Kieran was standing across the thoroughfare. He had a silly grin on his face. I thanked the remaining fans for coming out and shook a few hands. Then I exited through the side door of the booth.

"Thanks for waiting," I said.

"It was fun to watch. They were so excited to meet you."

I shrugged. "It's weird for me that people love the books so much. I write what I like to read, but the fun part is that they like them, too. I always get a bad case of impostor syndrome during signings. It never feels quite real."

"But you've written so many books." He seemed genuinely surprised.

"And with every novel I think: Maybe this is the time they figure out I have no idea what I'm doing."

"You do it so well. I find that hard to believe."

"It's true, though. Success doesn't necessarily bring confidence with it. Often, it just puts more pressure on the writer to do it again. I can't think about any of that when I'm writing."

"Here was I thinking that you just sat down, and it flowed right out through your fingers." He smiled.

"Some days. Others the struggle is real. So, what should we do first?"

"Are you hungry?"

I nodded. "You've met me. I can always eat."

"It's one of the things I like best about you."

I'm certain I blushed. Thankfully, the sun was going down, so hopefully he didn't notice.

We headed over to Rob's food truck, which was parked just off the jetty. My friend had jumped through so many hoops to get his license, and his truck had become a huge success. Mainly because his menu changed completely every time he opened the truck.

We stood in line, but when he saw us, Rob motioned us forward. I felt bad about cutting in line, but then he handed us two paper bags, along with some beverage cups.

"Kieran said you'd be stopping by, so I put these together for you. Enjoy." He winked at us.

Again, I felt the burn on my cheeks.

Why was everyone making such a big deal out of this? We were just two friends enjoying the fair.

We sat down at one of the picnic tables and discovered there were hand-held meat pies in the bags, along with a fruit salad, and the drinks were boba tea.

"Any news about the case since I last saw you?" I asked

"ME came back with the splinters in Declan's scalp. The type of wood is odd. They haven't figured that out yet. And it was swung upward, which means the assailant was shorter than he was."

"He was so tall and lanky, though, it could have been anyone. I'm guessing you haven't found the murder weapon?"

"No, we haven't. Though we'll be doing another search. We're waiting on the new warrants that basically give us permission to search wherever we need to out at the farm, the Donnels, the jewelry store, and the cottage where the mother has been staying."

"Do you think she could have killed her own child?"

He shrugged. "I've seen worse in my line of work. Until we find her and can question her, she is high on the suspect list." He grinned.

"What?"

"We don't have to talk about work tonight," he said. "It's okay to take a break."

I started to ask him why but stopped myself. "Understood, but you've met my brain. It sometimes only has one track."

He laughed.

Some other folks sat down at our table. And it seemed like a change of subject may be warranted after all.

"Do you have any idea how many books you just signed?" he asked.

"I never keep count. It was enough that my hand will hurt tomorrow, but it is worth it. Bringing business into the bookstore is part of my job as a sister. Have you met the new interns?"

"I have no idea how my sister found them, but they are all so knowledgeable about books. I'm quite impressed."

"Your sister seems to draw good people to her," he said.

"Unlike me, who ends up in trouble all the time?" I asked.

He laughed. "Don't put words into my mouth. I never said such a thing."

"Oh, you have. Many times." I sighed. "And you aren't wrong."

After we finished our meal, we disposed of the trash.

"Where should we head next? Do you like the rides?"

"I do. Usually, the faster the better, but not right after I eat. How do you feel about the Ferris wheel?"

"That would be grand. I think you'll like the view."

We headed over to a ticket booth where he purchased the tickets.

"Let me give you some money." I went to reach for my crossbody purse.

He held up a hand. "My treat tonight. Okay?"

"Sure." I shrugged.

The line for the Ferris wheel moved quickly. We climbed in, and then we were off. Making a few stops to let others onto the ride. When we reached the top, I gasped. "Shamrock Cove is gorgeous."

The whole place was lit up with twinkly lights on all the buildings. And the gas streetlamps added the perfect ambiance.

"It is," he said softly. But when I turned to look at him, his eyes were on me.

Cue the deep blush that I couldn't stop. That was happening a lot.

I glanced away and stared down at the ground. And then my phone, which was in my pocket, dinged at the same time that Kieran's rang.

We laughed.

It was a text from my sister.

The mother is here.

I couldn't see the booth from our angle. I texted back.

Keep her there.

"I'll be there as soon as I can," Kieran said. He had a stern look on his face.

"What is it?" I asked.

"Mr. Flynn may be coming around. He blinked his eyes open, but he seems out of it again. They've been pulling back on the drugs they gave him to help reduce the swelling on his brain."

"You should go."

"I'm surprised you don't want to come with me?"

"Lizzie texted and she needs me." I didn't want to tell him about the mother, in case she left before I arrived. I hoped I could talk her into going straight to the police. Besides, he was rushed, and I could handle this on my own.

When we reached the bottom of the Ferris wheel, he flashed his badge. The carnie let us off.

"I'll catch up with you later," I said. "Good luck."

"Sorry this was cut short," he said.

"Don't be. It's your job. And this might be the big break you've needed."

We rushed away. There were tons of people all over the grounds. That was good for business, not so much for my anxiety of being surrounding by too many bodies at once.

I tried to focus on what I would ask the mother.

As I neared the booth, my sister waved. The woman in front of her had dark-red hair. When she turned, I was surprised to find Belinda's lookalike. Though this version wore a lot of makeup, a leopard-skin blouse and leggings to match. Except for a few more lines around the eyes, the pair could have been twins.

"Mercy, I want you to meet Moira Brighton. She's an actress who just told me she has always wanted to write a book about her life. I told her about you. She wants to ask you a few questions." My sister's voice was light and casual. How she managed this sort of thing, I would never know. But she was good at it.

"I'd be happy to," I said. "I have a few minutes right now, if you'd like to chat."

The woman smiled. "That would be grand."

We found an empty picnic table and sat down. She was across from me, and it was uncanny how much she looked like Belinda up close. They could definitely have been sisters. Whatever she'd done through the years, she must have taken great care with her skin.

"Your sister says you are a famous author. So what are you doing living in Shamrock Cove?" she asked. And she didn't pull back on the rudeness.

I smiled. "It's a charming small town and quite different from Manhattan. And we took over our grandfather's bookstore."

"Wait. I remember him. Mr. O'Heyne, right?"

I nodded.

"He was kind to me when I was a kid," she said. "My parents weren't the best, so I spent a lot of time outside the house. He used to let me read all the American authors. That's why I wanted to be an actress. I'd read the books. Watched the movies." She sounded wistful.

But this woman had left her small children to chase her dream. I would not feel sorry for you.

"And did you go to America?" I asked.

She smirked. "For a bit. Did go to London for a time. I did some theater and commercials over the years. Though I sent many an audition tape overseas, things didn't work out that way."

"So, you want to write a memoir?"

She laughed. "Between you and me, I've lived a very interesting life. I think people would love to see behind the curtain of an actress."

I nodded. Not trusting myself to speak.

"I've thought about it many times, but I don't really know how to begin. Do you have some ideas for me?"

"Well, I'd start by making notes. Usually, memoirs are chronological, so your early life as a child. Then as a young adult. Do you have any interesting stories about the latter?"

"Being a young adult? Well, I was a child bride. Only eighteen when I married and had two children in two years," she said. "I wasn't ready for any of it. I think that is something other women could relate to, don't you think?"

"Perhaps. Do your children live here? What was it like raising them while going after your dreams?" Sometimes I was quite adept at playing dumb.

Her face screwed up. "My husband did most of the caring. I was traveling so much at the time."

Liar.

I disliked her so much, but I continued to pretend. "That must have been rough on all involved."

"You have no idea," she said dramatically.

"So, does your family still live here?"

She sniffed and pulled a tissue from her oversized bag. She dabbed her eyes. "I've recently lost my sweet son. I may never forgive myself for not coming back sooner to smooth things over with him."

The tears were as fake as the sentiment. Maybe she was a better actress than I'd thought.

"You said you had two children?"

"My other one is a daughter. She's dealing with a lot. I haven't wanted to bug her." That might have been the kindest thing she'd said so far.

"If she's going through a tough time, wouldn't it help to have her mother?"

She shrugged. "Perhaps. But there would be a great deal of drama involved, and I don't think I'm up for that right now. You know, so soon after losing my dear boy." Her eyes shifted, and she didn't appear to be sad at all.

This woman only thought of herself.

"How long have you been back in Shamrock Cove?"

She glanced up at the sky. "I've been staying in one of the summer cottages for a few weeks. My boyfriend has been looking to make some property deals here. So, I've been here to keep him entertained. One thing that hasn't changed is this town is so boring."

I could not have disagreed more.

"It's a shame you haven't had a chance to see your children, or your ex."

"I guess," she said. "Like I said, I wish I'd been able to at least speak to my son before he died." She dabbed her eyes again, but there were no tears.

I was having trouble remembering if this lack of empathy made her a psychopath or a sociopath. Either way, I completely believed her capable of murder. If she didn't break one of her long hot-pink nails.

"My ex... that's a long story, but you're right. It would add some drama to the book. Though, he's in the hospital, which is where my daughter is spending all her time. They say someone tried to kill him, but I don't believe it. He's always been able to hold his own and is hard-headed."

I remembered her letters begging to come home. Probably, she'd run out of money or it was linked in some way to Mac Bannon trying to buy the shop. Mr. Flynn had been smart to keep this woman away from his children.

When Lizzie and I had been younger, I sometimes wondered if that was why Mom didn't let us get to know our dad. Now I knew the truth, that he'd disappeared off the face of the earth.

If he was alive, I just didn't understand why he didn't come forward.

Her phone beeped. She glanced at it. "Oh, that's my Mac. I need to meet up with him. Thanks for your advice. You're a doll." She walked away teetering on her high heels.

Ugh. I tried not to judge people. Honestly. But that woman was a parasite. I couldn't imagine what poor Mr. Flynn had seen in her.

I texted Kieran to see if he was at the hospital. He was. Mr. Flynn hadn't woken up again.

I texted him.

I have so much to tell you.

I stopped by the booth to tell Lizzie I was headed to the hospital.

"You shouldn't go by yourself."

"There are tons of people in town. Safety in numbers," I said. "You make sure, though, that someone walks you and Mr. Poe home tonight."

"No."

"Wait. What?"

"I have a connection with Belinda. She's become a dear friend. If she's going through something, I want to be there. The interns can man the booth until closing, which is only two hours from now."

"But it's only their first day."

"Technically, second," she said. "And they are brilliant."

I glanced over to find them all smiling at her. She was quite good at getting people to love her and it looked like that had already happened. From their looks—even the serious Justin— they would have done anything for her.

"What about Mr. Poe?"

"We can bring him to you," Ronda chimed in. "He can stay with us until you're finished with your friend. Or you come get him at ours. Whatever works best for you."

"She's right," Rikki added. "We adore him." She was holding our dog, and he licked her cheek right on cue.

"Okay," I said. "Let's go."

We headed up Main Street.

Kieran wouldn't be happy about me having talked to a suspect on my own.

But he would have to get over it.

TWENTY-FOUR

As we were walking through town, that familiar feeling that we were being watched passed through me. Lizzie and I stopped at the same time.

"You feel it?" I whispered.

She nodded slightly. We turned quickly to catch whoever watched us. But there were so many people walking up and down the street, it was impossible to see anyone clearly in the dark. Even with the twinkling lights and gas lamps, there were shadows along the way.

"That was weird," she said.

"It was. I'm glad to know it isn't my paranoia."

"No. I sensed it. Must be a twin thing."

We never questioned those moments when we shared something so simpatico. We'd been doing it all our lives.

"Do you think it might be..."

"I don't know. If it is, why doesn't he come forward?"

"Maybe, like the actress, he is afraid we might not like him for disappearing," Lizzie said.

"But maybe the truth isn't so simple," I said. "I can't see

Mom falling in love with a narcissist. She was too smart for that," I said.

"True. But you and I know how hurt she had been. Think about it. She seldom dated. I always thought she was still in love with him."

I shrugged. "She never really said. But if he was so great, why isn't he coming forward now? And is it really him? It could be my stalker followed us across the pond."

She shivered and pulled her cardigan tighter. "I hope not. That's going to make me really paranoid."

"Same," I said.

"It's more romantic to think it might be our long-lost father. A regular scary stalker makes our lives more of a thriller."

I laughed. "You aren't wrong."

We hurried up to the hospital. When we made our way down the hall, Kieran was standing outside the ward speaking to his team member on duty. When he glanced down the hall, he waved us forward.

"What happened?" I asked.

"He's back in a coma," Kieran said. "But when he roused, he only said one name."

"Don't keep us in suspense. What was it?"

"Moira," he said. "He called out for his ex-wife."

So many thoughts flooded my brain I missed what Kieran said next. Then my sister was talking.

She put a hand on my arm. "Mercy, tell him. I'm going to check on Belinda."

"Tell me what?" Kieran asked.

He motioned for me to sit down on the bench down the hallway. "What happened?"

"I bumped into Moira."

"Why didn't you tell me? We have a BOLO out on her."

"It happened fast, and then she left quickly. I was going to tell you, but I didn't want to interrupt what you had going on here."

"Were you really going to tell me?"

"Yes," I said vehemently. "She really didn't give much away except that she was here at the time of the attack and the murder. She's been in town for a few weeks. And she's been working with her boyfriend. I wouldn't put it past her to have done both crimes. She says she wanted to reach out to her kids, yet she hasn't done so. I don't believe a word she said. I'm telling you she attacked one or both."

He jerked back. "Do you have proof and motive? Did she happen to confess?"

I sighed. "No. But you're going to bring her in, right?"

"Like I said, there is a BOLO out."

"She said she was headed home," I said. "She claimed that Bannon texted her from the cottage."

Kieran frowned.

"What?"

"After we questioned him, Bannon and his lawyer headed back to Dublin. He isn't in town."

"Then who texted her? That's weird, right? She doesn't know me, why would she lie?"

He shrugged.

I snapped my fingers. I had an idea. I headed to the front desk. The nurse there was a customer at the bookstore.

"Lily, right?"

"Yes. It's good to see you again, Mercy."

"I think we chatted at the bookshop not long ago. You came in for the new Jodi Thomas. You love your cowboys."

She grinned. "That's right. Can I help you?"

I pulled my phone out of my pocket. "By chance has this woman come in during Mr. Flynn's stay?"

She nodded. "She has. Said she was his wife. That they were estranged, but she asked to be updated on his condition.

She asked that I call if and when something happened. We have a family policy, and we do that for them. Why? Did I do something wrong?"

"Did you just reach out to her?"

She nodded. "I sent a text that he woke up and called for her."

Kieran and I glanced at each other.

"You didn't answer. Did I do something wrong?"

"No. Not at all."

Kieran was on his radio calling for a roadblock.

If she killed him, and thought he was waking up—she'd be trying to make a run for it.

I ran out of the hospital. Without thinking, I headed to the train station around the corner. There were a ton of people waiting for the last train out of town for the night.

I stood up on one of the benches to see over the crowd. People stared at me like I'd lost my mind. But I saw her. That red hair was unmistakable. I pushed through the crowds.

"Where are you going, Moira?" I asked.

She jumped, but then quickly reach a hand up to smooth her hair. "Back to Dublin. There is nothing for me here."

"What about your daughter, Belinda? Don't you think she could use some comforting from her mother."

She narrowed her eyes. "I never told you her name."

"My sister and I are friends with her, and I've been helping the police with their inquiries. I'll need you to come back to the station with me."

"You're not the police. I'm not going anywhere with you."

The crowd around us took a few steps back watching the interplay with interest.

"I'm afraid you're wrong about that. As I said, I'm working with the police as a consultant. You need to come with me."

As I gently tugged on her arm, she shoved me off her.

I stumbled back. Directly in front of the oncoming train.

TWENTY-FIVE

One minute my arms became a windmill trying to find purchase as I fell toward the track. The light from the train blinded me. The next second, I face-planted into the hard-concrete floor, my right arm feeling as though it had been pulled from the socket. Then something landed on top of me, squeezing the last of my breath out.

Everything on my body hurt and I couldn't turn my head.

"Mercy, are you okay?" The weight lifted, and then Kieran flipped me over onto my back. "Tell me where you are hurt."

"Everywhere," I whispered. I still had no breath.

"I didn't push her," Moira said loudly.

Sheila was in the middle of handcuffing the woman and cautioning her.

"Save it for the interview," Sheila said roughly. She pulled the woman away.

Kieran was still beside me. "Do you think you can sit up?"

"No. I'm good here." I still had a hard time breathing. "Did you land on top of me?"

"I was scared to death and yanked a bit too hard and threw us both off balance."

"S'okay. Better than being smashed by a train."

"There is that," he agreed. "Scared the life from me, you did. I've aged twenty years."

"You still look okay," I whispered.

He snorted and then grinned.

One of the EMTs ran up to me. Another one pushed a gurney. That's when I realized there was a huge crowd around us.

"Tommy, get Greg and talk to the witnesses," he said. He turned to the onlookers. "The train won't leave until we have statements from everyone," he shouted. "Please cooperate with my officers. It will cut down on your delay."

The two paramedics rolled me onto a board, and then the gurney. "This isn't necessary," I said breathlessly. But my chest was tight, and I struggled to breathe right.

"You don't know that," Kieran said. "You fell hard, with my weight on top of you. There could be broken bones. You'll need scans at the hospital."

I groaned. "You know I don't like that place."

"We just need to check you out, miss," the EMT said. "You took a hard fall from what the detective inspector says."

I sighed.

"I need to get a statement from you, but let's get you seen to first," Kieran said.

I nodded. My head hurt and I reached a hand up. There was something sticky in my hair. When I saw my hand, there was blood on it.

"Oh."

One of the EMTs cleaned off my hand with a wipe.

"Let's keep your hands to your sides until we get your scans. We don't want to risk further injury or infection," he said.

"I'm fine," I said again.

"We'll see," Kieran said beside me as they wheeled me out.

Then we were in the ambulance, which made a very short jaunt around the corner to the hospital.

When we arrived, my sister waited there at the glass door with her worried face on. "What did you do now?" she screeched. "You're covered in blood." She was crying and worried. She really wasn't much of a screecher. I'd probably scared the heck out of her.

"I fell. You know I'm a klutz."

"Don't make me laugh. I'm mad at you," she said. "Kieran texted. I thought you were dead."

"Kieran." I sighed.

"I just said we were bringing you in," he said.

"You look like death," she said. "And your head is bleeding like a bloody faucet."

I laughed and then winced.

"Why are you laughing?"

"You sounded British for a minute. All those UK mysteries I make you watch are paying off."

She grunted. "I'm glad you think you are a comic. Is she going to be okay?" she asked the EMT.

"Let's get her into emergency one," a new voice said.

My groupies tried to follow us into the room, but one of the male nurses stopped them at the door.

A man came forward with a bright light. "I'm Doctor Franklin," he said. "Can you tell me your name."

"Mercy McCarthy," I said.

"The writer?"

I sighed. "Yep. That's me."

"Well, looks like you were involved in one of your own plot lines. Let's get you checked out." He flashed the light in my eyes again. "Injury to the front, right temple. Possible concussion. Dislocated right shoulder." He pressed down on my right ribs, and I cried out. "We'll need a chest scan." He moved down my body pushing and probing.

"All right then. First up, we'll see to that head wound. They tend to bleed a lot, but we'll get a scan to make sure there is no brain damage."

I started to make a joke, but I kept it to myself.

They worked on my head.

"What is your pain level?" he asked as he finished the sutures on what I thought was my forehead. They'd given me numbing shots so I couldn't really tell. "I need to know from one to ten."

"A five?" That was a lie. It felt like an eleven, but I didn't want to be a whiner.

He chuckled.

"What?"

"You're one of those," he said.

"One of what?"

"Tough guys. Or tough woman, in your case. That dislocated shoulder alone would have most grown men passing out."

"Shouldn't you put it back where it goes?"

He laughed again. "We will. You're going for some scans. Once we've looked at all those, we'll start putting you back together."

"Right. Can you do me a favor?"

"What's that?"

"Tell my sister everything is going to be okay. I don't want her to worry. She's been through a lot. I don't like scaring her."

"That I can do. But before that I'm giving you something for the pain that I know is at least an eleven."

"You're pretty smart," I said. And then there was warmth soaking through my body. I was so very sleepy, and I sank into the blackness.

When I woke up, I was in the hospital. That wasn't much of a surprise. The fact that my sister was on one side of the bed, Mr.

Poe lay at my feet, and Kieran was asleep in a chair on the right side, was funny.

"How did you get in here?" I whispered to Mr. Poe, who had lifted his head. He carefully climbed up beside me.

I tried to sit up straight and grunted. My ribs and my shoulder felt like someone had done a number on my bones.

Grunting woke up my guests.

"You're awake," Lizzie said. "I was beginning to worry."

"Why does the top half of my body feel like I've been through a meat grinder?"

Lizzie had tears dripping down her cheeks. Kieran handed her a hanky. I didn't even know he carried one.

"They put your shoulder back in, and you have a couple of cracked ribs. Your head will take a while to heal, but you don't have a concussion," Kieran said. "Sorry about it all, part of this is my fault."

"Don't do that," Lizzie said. "I heard what happened. You saved her from that horrible woman. If she's a bit sore, it's her fault for running after bad people like she's some kind of superhero."

She turned to me. "Do you know how lucky you are? How close you came to death? Do you have any consideration as to what it would have been like for me if something had happened to you?" Her voice was becoming more high-pitched.

"Lizzie," I said softly.

"What?" She sniffed.

"I'm okay. I'm really okay."

She pointed a finger at me. "Only because Kieran was there to save your life."

I turned to him. "Thanks for that," I said.

"You are welcome. But your sister makes a good point. You're lucky I followed you."

"I didn't think she'd try to shove me in front of a train. I was just trying to keep her from getting on to it. And, honestly, I don't think she actually shoved me. She was pulling away, and then the force of that—"

"Sent you hurtling in front of a train," Kieran finished.

"That might have been one of the scariest moments of my life."

"Good," my sister said. "Maybe it will put some sense into you."

I smiled.

"Why are you smiling? I'm still very angry with you."

"Now, you sound like Mom."

She rolled her eyes.

"So, did she admit to everything?"

Kieran shook his head. "She swears she had nothing to do with the death of her son. But she did break into the clock store. She was looking for things to sell. She didn't think anyone would be there. Bannon refused to get her a lawyer, so she'll be looking at some prison time when all is said and done."

"Did she hurt Mr. Flynn?"

"Says when he saw her, he seized up. Fell forward and hit the cabinet on his way down. But she left him there. A jury won't look kindly on that."

"Good," I said. "But then who killed Declan?"

"I'll figure that out. You focus on getting well," he said.

Like that was going to happen. I snapped my fingers, and something clicked in my head.

"The cricket bat. Could it have been a paddle? It's sort of the same shape as an oar."

"Where are you going with this?"

"When we searched the boat and found the jewels, I remember something was missing from the wall. What if he was attacked on the boat, and then stumbled his way up the hill? Maybe he didn't realize how hurt he was."

Yes. Something in my gut told me I was right about this.

"We searched the boat, and all we found were the jewels."

"Right, but if the murder weapon is missing, they couldn't have checked it thoroughly. Your team is good, but the attack could have even happened on the dock. Have them look for blood. When they were stitching me up, the doctor said head wounds bleed a lot. We had so much rain though. They might not find much."

"I'll investigate it. Wood tends to hold onto DNA. Promise me, you'll stay here and heal."

"Promise. But you need to look at Jessie and her dad. Either he found out what happened, or she and Declan had a fight."

"What makes you think it is one of them?"

"My gut. But you need evidence. I think it is on the boat or it has been hidden somewhere nearby. And if you can find that oar or paddle..."

My sister sighed. "You never stop, do you?"

"My brain isn't like yours," I said.

"Right. Mine doesn't cause me bodily harm."

"I'll look into this. Remember, she's healing, Lizzie. Maybe hold off on the fisticuffs until she's better."

My sister rolled her eyes at him.

He left.

And then the doctor came in. Lizzie sat up straighter and smoothed her hair down around her face.

What is that about?

"Hello, Doctor Franklin," she said sweetly. Her attitude had done a 180.

"I told you to call me Angus," he said. He was quite handsome with dark hair, a sprinkling of gray at the temples.

"Angus, as you can see, she is awake."

I glanced at them like I was in a tennis match. Were my sister and the doctor flirting? That was interesting.

"So I heard from the detective inspector." He smiled down at me. "How are you feeling?"

"I'm awake. Pretty much everything hurts."

He nodded. "It will be a few weeks before you feel like running after criminals again."

I made a face. "So you heard about that?"

"It was on the newspaper's website. I think the headline was 'Famous Author Thrown in Front of Train'."

I snorted. "A bit sensationalist."

"I agree though, from what I understand, also the truth."

"Any chance I can get out of here if I promise to be a model patient?"

"That can be arranged. But you'll need to have those ribs rewrapped in a few days. And the stiches out in a few weeks."

"She will keep her appointments," Lizzie said. And then she gave me a look.

"What she said," I grumbled.

Angus laughed.

"Thank you for putting me back together," I said.

"As I told your sister, it's my job. I'll send in the nurse with your paperwork, but we'll get you out of here."

He left.

"I know you're mad at me, but I have a burning question," I said.

"What's that?"

"How did you sneak Mr. Poe in here?"

"Angus told the administrator he was our emotional support dog. They couldn't say no."

I rubbed his chin.

"Well, it wasn't a lie."

"True."

"Mercy, please stop putting your life in danger," she said softly.

"I didn't think I was. I was in a train station full of people. I just had to keep her off that train. I had a feeling if she got on, we'd never see her again."

"Still."

"You like Angus," I said, changing the subject.

Her cheeks became a bright red. We shared that dumb blushing gene.

"He's been very kind. And he's checked on you often."

"You mean while I was passed out? Are you certain he wasn't here to see you?"

She appeared to be surprised, but then she glanced at the door and smiled.

The door opened and a male nurse bustled in. "I hear you are outta here," he said jovially and plopped some papers down on the table beside my bed.

"Where do I sign?"

TWENTY-SIX

A few days later, I sat in Kieran's office. He'd allowed me to sit and watch his interviews with the Simmons family. First up was Jessie. She'd been crying. I wondered what was going on. Though, she had every right to be sad about the death of her fiancé.

She sat down with her solicitor, and then Kieran walked in, again with a thick file folder.

He pushed the button on the recorder and announced himself and everyone in the room. "Jessie, do you have anything you would like to tell me before we begin?"

She shook her head.

"For the recording the suspect shook her head. In the future, I'll need you to answer," he said firmly.

She sniffed. "No comment."

"Right. I'd like you to take me through the events on the day Declan died. I need to know where you were when you returned to town. Did you go to his boat?"

She glanced at the lawyer who nodded.

"Yes."

"And did you and Declan have an argument over coming back to town?"

Her eyes went wide. "I don't know what you mean."

He pushed a picture of something across to her.

"Do you recognize this?"

She shrugged.

"Please speak up for the recording."

"It's a paddle. I've seen a lot of them."

"Yes, but this particular one has your fingerprints on it. It is from Declan's boat."

"So? I've already said I was on there." Her eye's widened, and then she ducked her head. That was suspicious.

"Your fingerprints are on the flat end of the paddle. Odd, right? Why would you be holding it from the wrong end?"

"I was probably helping to clean up or something. He wasn't very neat. I was always cleaning up after him."

"Okay. So do you admit to cleaning the blood off the handle?"

Her eyes went wide.

"Someone tried to bleach it, but wood holds onto blood and DNA. This was the murder weapon that killed your fiancé."

No one said a word, and then she sobbed.

"I didn't mean to hurt him," she said. "He said we couldn't leave. That he had to take care of his sister, now that his dad might never wake up. But he didn't understand. I'd broken all ties with my father. I couldn't stay here. I'd given everything up for him. He didn't seem to care about that. I just wanted him to listen to me."

Kieran really was good at this. I had no right to feel pride, but I did.

"So, you struck him."

"I swung it around. He laughed at me. Then he left the boat. I had no idea I'd... I didn't know that I'd made contact. He laughed it off like it was nothing. I didn't mean to kill him. I loved him."

Then the sobs wouldn't stop.

Kieran turned off the recorder and left the room. When he came into the office, I grinned. "You're really good at your job."

"I'm better with your help," he admitted. "It was brilliant about the paddle."

"You would have come around to it. I was inspired by my own head injury and the idea that I could have walked around without realizing it for some time. So weird that Declan dies from that, and his dad—wait, how is his dad?"

"He woke up this morning," he said. "Docs think he has a long recovery ahead and there is worry about strokes, given the damage he sustained to his heart and brain. But he's alive."

I blew out a breath.

He glanced at his watch and frowned.

"What's wrong?"

"We need to go," he said.

"Don't you have to interview the father, Mr. Simmons? He may have helped her."

"Already have."

"Then why... Kieran, was this a diversion so that my sister could set up some sort of surprise party? It's party time, isn't it?"

He shrugged. "I have no idea what you're talking about. All I know is if I don't have you to the back room of the Crown and Clover in ten minutes, my grandmother and your sister will kill me."

"Ugh. I hate surprise parties."

"I'm not much of a fan myself."

"I need to stop by the house and get her gift."

"That can be arranged. I'll run in and get it, since you're still moving slowly."

"Deal. And thanks for being a good sport. I can't believe they coerced you like this."

"When your sister and my grandmother get together, it is impossible to say no."

I laughed.

After a quick stop by our house—where Kieran ran in and picked up my sister's gift from my office—we headed to the pub.

He parked the car and then put a hand on my arm.

"What is it? I promise to act surprised."

"It's not that. Uh…" He seemed worried about something.

"You can tell me anything," I said softly, and I meant it. We'd grown close.

"Nothing is wrong. I was wondering, since you are injured, if you still wanted to go to the dance at the fête with me."

The heat on my cheeks burned. "Oh. Yes. I mean, I'm not sure how much dancing I could do but I'd like doing that. Um. With you."

We sat their grinning at each other.

"Do you think we'll ever get my mom's watch back?" I blurted out.

He laughed as if understanding my need to change the subject quickly. "After the cases are tried, it will be returned. But that could be a year or more."

Then he jumped out of the SUV and ran around to open my door for me.

"Thank you."

He nodded. Then he tucked my good arm in his. The other one was still in a sling while my shoulder healed. Surprisingly, there was a sign on the door that the pub was closed for a private party.

My sister must have rented the whole place.

We paused just outside the door of the back room.

"Are you ready?"

"No."

The doors opened and everyone I knew in Shamrock Cove yelled, 'Surprise!' I started laughing and I couldn't stop, even when it hurt my sore ribs. Mr. Poe ran forward and jumped up and down excitedly.

As I glanced around the room at the smiling, happy faces, I couldn't stop grinning. Maybe I didn't like parties, but even I had to admit I was incredibly blessed. I was surrounded by people I had grown to love like family. And I was part of the fabric of this town. I'd never felt so loved.

There was cake, wine, beer, and lots of appetizers from Matt and Rob. It was one of the best parties I'd ever been to, and it was for me and my twin. The chatter was loud and there were so many smiles.

It felt like the Grinch's heart was swelling with love.

These are my people. And I was theirs. I would do anything to protect every single one of them.

A LETTER FROM LUCY CONNELLY

Wonderful reader,

Thank you for supporting this series and reading *Murder on the Clock*. If you enjoy the series and want to keep up with the latest, please sign up on the following link. Your email will never be shared, and you can unsubscribe at any time.

www.bookouture.com/lucy-connelly

I so adore having the opportunity to write these stories set in Shamrock Cove. And though it may seem silly, Mercy and Lizzie have become like family to me. I look forward to writing about their relationship and their adventures. Like you, I'm always curious to see what they do next.

I'd love to hear from you. Please follow me on social media or on my website. Oh, and I'm so grateful for your amazing and insightful reviews.

Love to you all,

Lucy Connelly

KEEP IN TOUCH WITH LUCY

www.lucyconnelly.com

facebook.com/LucyConnellyBooks

x.com/candacehavens

instagram.com/candace_havens

ACKNOWLEDGMENTS

I'm so grateful to you, readers. Thank you for the support of this series. These books would not be what they are without my amazing editors, Ruth Tross and Brittany Golob. You are both so insightful. And to the team at Bookouture, from marketing and PR, to sales and everyone in between, thank you for everything. You make working with your team absolutely amazing.

My agent Jill Marsal is as patient as they come and has guided me as an author all along the way. I will never be able to thank you enough.

And back to you, dear readers. I get a bit weepy when I think of your many emails and encouraging words. I could not travel this path without you, my friends.

PUBLISHING TEAM

Turning a manuscript into a book requires the efforts of many people. The publishing team at Bookouture would like to acknowledge everyone who contributed to this publication.

Audio
Alba Proko
Sinead O'Connor
Melissa Tran

Commercial
Lauren Morrissette
Hannah Richmond
Imogen Allport

Cover design
Lisa Horton

Data and analysis
Mark Alder
Mohamed Bussuri

Editorial
Brittany Golob
Ria Clare

Copyeditor
Jane Eastgate

Proofreader
Anne O'Brien

Marketing
Alex Crow
Melanie Price
Occy Carr
Ciara Rosney
Martyna Młynarska

Operations and distribution
Marina Valles
Stephanie Straub
Joe Morris

Production
Hannah Snetsinger
Mandy Kullar
Nadia Michael
Charlotte Hegley

Publicity
Kim Nash
Noelle Holten
Jess Readett
Sarah Hardy

Rights and contracts
Peta Nightingale
Richard King
Saidah Graham

Dear Reader,

We'd love your attention for one more page to tell you about the crisis in children's reading, and what we can all do.

Studies have shown that reading for fun is the **single biggest predictor of a child's future life chances** – more than family circumstance, parents' educational background or income. It improves academic results, mental health, wealth, communication skills, ambition and happiness.

The number of children reading for fun is in rapid decline. Young people have a lot of competition for their time, and a worryingly high number do not have a single book at home.

Hachette works extensively with schools, libraries and literacy charities, but here are some ways we can all raise more readers:

- Reading to children for just 10 minutes a day makes a difference
- Don't give up if children aren't regular readers – there will be books for them!

- Visit bookshops and libraries to get recommendations
- Encourage them to listen to audiobooks
- Support school libraries
- Give books as gifts

There's a lot more information about how to encourage children to read on our websites: **www.RaisingReaders.co.uk** and **www.JoinRaisingReaders.com**.

Thank you for reading.